50p

ƎR

Deathwater

Darkwater is a historical home still owned by the Forrests, the pioneer family whose founder built it in colonial times. Journalist Bob Slater, who is writing an article about the house and family for a local paper, is killed in a car accident on a dark, wet night in the steep and dangerous Kaye Street, so children's author Micky Douglas agrees to finish the article.

But Bob's death bears an uncanny resemblance to that of William, son of the autocratic Eileen Forrest, in the same spot sixteen years previously, and, after finding a cryptic message doodled by Bob Slater shortly before he died, Micky begins to wonder just how 'accidental' both deaths really were.

Driven by curiosity, Micky sets out to investigate and, in spite of being warned by his friend, Inspector Reeves, uncovers a deadly plot to suppress an old scandal of Government and police corruption, the truth about the supposed suicide of Eileen Forrest's husband, a horrific crime against the original native tribe which once inhabited the Darkwater land—and a cunning murderer who is determined to remove Micky before he discovers the truth.

ANNE INFANTE

Deathwater

THE CRIME CLUB
An Imprint of HarperCollins *Publishers*

First published in Great Britain in 1991
by The Crime Club, an imprint of
HarperCollins Publishers, 77–85 Fulham Palace Road,
Hammersmith, London W6 8JB

Anne Infante asserts the moral right to be identified
as the author of this work.

© Anne Infante 1991

British Library Cataloguing in Publication Data

Infante, Anne
    Deathwater.
    I. Title
    823

ISBN 0 00 232333 8

Photoset in Linotron Baskerville by
Rowland Phototypesetting Ltd
Bury St Edmunds, Suffolk
Printed in Great Britain by
Harper Collins Book Manufacturing, Glasgow

AUTHOR'S NOTE

Aboriginals in the Brisbane Area, a paper by F. S. Colliver and
F. P. Woolston, published by the Archaeology Branch,
Department of Community Services, 1986, states that by
1860 the North Brisbane aboriginal tribe, once number-
ing 300, was extinct, except for some still living at
Mooloolabah.

I have no reason whatever to doubt the veracity of this
statement. *Deathwater* is, after all, only a story.

Anne Infante
Brisbane, 1990

CHAPTER 1

Carnation Belle Douglas gave a hollow wail which made me jump nearly out of my skin. I looked severely across at where she was sitting on the window-ledge. She looked back with a steady, unblinking gaze. Stalemate!

I was in full flight with my typewriter and not inclined to be deflected from my purpose. Last time I had surfaced to full consciousness, the rain had been roaring on the roof in a solid downpour and Carnie had been amusing herself chasing any stray drops that trickled down the outside of the window, covering them triumphantly with her paws only to watch, puzzled, as they slid out from under and continued their downward way on the opposite side of the glass. Now her look was frankly bored.

'In a minute, Carnie,' I promised vaguely and turned back to creation.

I was roused again some time later by the dread sound of claws in furniture and swung around to see my flatmate using the back of the sofa as a tree. I yelled and she froze, then gave me back a limpid look, full of innocence.

'Who, me?' her candid eyes said. '*Me* misbehave?'

Confident now that she had my full attention, she leaped gracefully to the floor and with an anxious look sat, dog-like, with her nose against the door.

'No!' I told her firmly. 'We've played that game enough. You don't need to go outside and it's bucketing down. Use the litter tray in the bathroom, if you're desperate.'

Ignoring such an ill-mannered remark, she raised herself on her hind legs and scrabbled urgently at the door with her front paws. Scrape, scrabble, scratch . . .

'Carnie!' I shouted, exasperated. But I got up and went to the door with a sigh.

We'd been through this pantomime several times already today, and countless times over the past dripping week. It goes like this. Carnie trots ahead of me, casting an occasional eye over her shoulder to see if I'm coming. She goes down the stairs from my attic flat to the front door of the red-brick Victorian house where we live and says very clearly:

'I want to go out now.'

I open the door. She looks taken aback at the steady wall of water falling on the front steps.

'Oh!' she says, twitching her tail in perturbation. Then she has the solution. As I close the door she trots down the passage to the back door. I open it. She is greeted by a similar downpour. She looks at me accusingly, as if I have personally arranged this for her discomfort.

'But it's raining here, too,' her disgusted look informs me.

'Now you know!' I tell her and she turns an offended back and stalks regally up the two flights of stairs to No. 5, where she proceeds to ignore me. For a while silence reigns and I can get back to work.

I joined in the umpteenth round of the game and followed her downstairs. We checked out the front door. It was raining out there! We checked out the back door. Surprise, surprise!

Later found me prowling restlessly about in my flat, feeling out of sorts and restricted. With all the windows shut, the air was close and humid and everything felt damp to the touch. The heavy rain drummed menacingly on the roof. I got the full sound effects, being the top flat. The mezzanine floor where I sleep is closer still, and I don't sleep well with rain like this. It makes me edgy, the threatening sound of it, although it's par for the course in April.

April rains. Our regular autumnal soaking, but usually there are some breaks, some almost bright days in between the deluges. Days when you can catch your breath, blink at the brightness behind thinning clouds, feel a watery sunbeam or two, say to chance met strangers, 'Looks like it's

clearing up at last!' This time we'd had almost no let-up for
a solid week, the rain merely switching from light showery
to heavy flooding and back. The odd days when it hadn't
rained the sky had hung, low and threatening, vindictively
blocking out the sun.

We Brisbaneites tend to get a little restive when it rains
for too long without stopping. For one thing, we're not used
to it. After all, this is the Sunshine State. For another, it's
too close for comfort to that January in '74 when we had
the last major floods and the Brisbane River forgot to remain
well-mannered within its banks and detoured through the
city instead, until the city buildings were standing knee-deep
in water and overseas headlines screamed, BRISBANE
ENTIRELY WASHED INTO THE SEA!, which piece of
over-enthusiastic reporting jammed the international phone
links for days. We get a major flood like that about once
every century. Well, if they would site the city on a swamp
what can you expect, right?

Already local flooding was growing, people in the outer
suburbs were getting cut off as gently innocent suburban
creeks became raging torrents, the main highway north was
cut in several places and shops and houses in the low-lying
areas were sandbagging to keep out the water. And I was
getting more and more restless.

'A walk!' I decided. 'Do me good to get out of the flat.' I
could pop up the road, have a moan about the weather in
Paddo's 7-to-7 and get Carnie some more cat food. And a
tin or two of her favourite milk. She was named for it and
it's her addiction. She was sulking on my desk now, clawing
in a desultory way at my papers.

'That's our bread and butter, love.' I removed her and
threw a cloth over the lot in case she tried again while I was
out. She's a great destroyer of manuscripts. A born critic.

At least the constant rain was keeping the temperatures
up. A preview of the Greenhouse Effect. I opened the front
door into the warm, heavy air and went cautiously out

under my trusty black umbrella. The rain had eased back to light showers as I splashed along the footpath. A car swished past, spraying up a plume of water; some storm-water drains had backed up. Luckily I move fast.

'Moron!' I groused after the car, and leaped back as it came to a sudden screeching halt and reversed at a danger-ous pace, water sheeting into the air around it.

A familiar voice shrieked, 'Micky!', the driver's door flew open and Joss Bates was clinging to me, her unruly dark curls wetting my shirt.

I recovered my balance and put an arm around her, trying to position the umbrella to cover us both—a fairly useless exercise. She was sopping, and transferring most of it to me.

Joss runs the *Paddington News*, a local surburban paper she produces twice weekly. She gathers the various articles and ads together, edits and pastes up the finished product and one of the big newspaper houses prints it. I write the occasional book review for her. Joss likes to appear tough. She's made it on her own in what was once very much a man's world and she can stand up to anyone. She's efficient, hides her feelings, is as undemonstrative as a church social. I'd never seen her cry before, let alone cling to me for support, shaking and defenceless, and I know her as well as anyone and better than most. She's more likely to swear, push a mere male out of her way and boot a problem out the door before it can draw breath.

Realizing the obvious enormity of whatever had hap-pened, I put her gently back from me and anxiously scanned her pale face. Her eyes looked huge and dark and red-rimmed from too many tears.

'Joss! What's wrong, love?'

She made a valiant effort to pull herself together. 'It's Bob, Bob Slater.' She cleared her throat huskily. 'He's— oh, Micky, he's dead!' Her lip trembled and her eyes welled again.

The shock surged through me, leaving me gaping stupidly. That wasn't possible. Why, only last week I'd run into Bob, and . . . 'Good God, Joss! How?'

'He was doing a story. That series about the colonial families in the area and the historical houses. He'd been to see an old lady who's the last of one of the pioneering families at Bardon. Well, you know Bob—always drives like a bloody maniac. He came too fast down Kaye Street and spun off the road. It must have been slippery with the wet. Went straight into the fence at the bottom of the Governor's place. He was unconscious when they dragged him out.' She gasped at the thought of it, and bit her lip. 'They called me—I was at the flat, waiting for him. I went straight to the hospital. Been there all night. The doctors thought he had a chance but he just went downhill in spite of all their efforts. He died at six o'clock this morning.'

'Oh, Joss, I'm sorry, love. God, poor old Bob.' I shook my head at the suddenness of it all. I liked Bob. He used to be a crime reporter with one of the big newspapers but the long hours, stress, and heavy drinking that went with the job took their toll on his family, then on him. His doctor advised him that giving it up would be conducive to continued life. He took the advice but couldn't entirely give up reporting, which was meat and drink to him, so he did freelance for his old paper and worked part-time for Joss. It was common knowledge that she and Bob were closer than they let on.

I looked down at her in silence, taking in the brightly checked Western-style shirt clinging wetly to her body and blue denim jeans tucked into high-heeled boots. Joss is a cowgirl at heart. Her dark hair curled in dripping rats' tails against her forehead. My heart lurched. She looked exhausted.

'You're drenched!' I held the umbrella helplessly over her.

'I went for a walk.' She looked at me, half defiantly. 'When they told me he was—he didn't make it, I just ran out and walked and walked. They wanted to know about Joanna, where she lived, if I knew her phone number. I told them she and Bob were estranged and they could ask the police, and high-tailed it out. I must have been walking for hours until I remembered I'd left the car at the hospital, so I went back for it. Then I thought of you, and just wanted— just needed . . .'

She tailed off. 'Oh, Joss.' I put my arm around her again, but this time she pushed me away. 'I'm all right. Don't know why I'm bothering you about it. I don't usually go to pieces and act like a drongo!'

'Come on.' I took her arm firmly and steered her towards her car. 'We're both sopping, you careless woman. Come back to my place and dry off, for heaven's sake. Have you eaten?'

'No, I'm not hungry.

'Bloody ridiculous!' I pushed her into the driver's seat and slammed the door on her, then joined her in the small green Mazda. 'Get a move on. You'll do yourself a damage staying in those wet things.'

I made Joss take a hot shower and her clothes clacked round in the drier as she made an attempt to eat the food I put in front of her. She sat, lost in my dressing-gown, a pathetic figure with a white, sad face and black shadows under her eyes. I bullied her into eating and made her drink some hot coffee, laced with a tot of brandy for comfort. Most of the time she answered in monosyllables, her mind far away.

When her clothes were dry she ran the iron over them half-heartedly and slipped into the bathroom to change. I poured myself another cuppa and was wondering what else I could do for her when she reappeared and fixed me with a determined stare.

'Micky, will you help me, please?'

'Of course,' I said readily. 'Anything I can do, love.'

'It's the story,' she said urgently, 'the story Bob was writing. He'd been on it for a few days, researching the place and the family. It's the last of the series and I've got no one to finish it. I wanted—well, it would be a shame if he'd put all that work in and it never got published.'

A memorial to Bob? I thought. Hell!

'I wondered if you'd follow it up; get his notes and finish anything that needed doing. After all, you're a writer.'

'Kids' books,' I said feebly, thinking of my unfinished manuscript waiting for attention. 'The odd book review for you. Not journalism.'

She stopped me with a look. 'Oh, Micky, don't be bloody wet!' Then she swung away from me and there was a minute or two of strained silence before she turned back and said in a gentler voice, 'Sorry, I didn't mean to dump on you, but there's nothing to it, really. It's just the story of the family and how they came to settle here and anyway, Bob will have done most of the work.'

'The thing is, I'm up to my ears already,' I pleaded, fully aware that I was losing the argument. 'I've a new book under way and a deadline to meet myself.'

'Micky, please! It would mean so much to me. You said you'd do anything. Surely you could manage—it's not a lot to ask.'

'I'll think about it,' I relented. Joss turned towards the door.

'I have to get back to the *News*,' she said flatly. 'The paper won't edit itself and I'm going to be short-handed, now.' Bob used to help her in the office when she was rushed. 'I've got a heap of proofs to go over.'

'You'd be better off going home for the rest of the day,' I protested.

'No, I need to have something to do. Otherwise I'd just be thinking about—thinking about—and if you won't do the article I'd better try to find someone else.'

Her eyes were overbright but she was composed. I made up my mind.

'Look, love, OK, I'll do Bob's story for you.'

It was an instinctive sympathetic gesture. I had no way of knowing what I was getting into.

CHAPTER 2

April was still raining as I waved Joss off. She'd promised to get me Bob's notes. He had a small flat ten minutes away and she assumed the unfinished article would be there. I knew they didn't live together, but she had a spare key to his flat so I could guess the rest. Joss lived, gipsy-style, in a caravan she parked on a friend's farm at Samford, a country suburb some 20 kilometres north of the city, but she often stayed overnight in town.

She rang me just before nine that night.

'Are you still at the *News*?' I was surprised. 'You're working late.'

'It's got to be done,' she said abruptly, then went on, sounding puzzled. 'Micky, I couldn't find Bob's notes or anything about the Bardon place. I went over right after I left you. He must have had a fair amount of material. He'd spent hours in the library and looking up old newspaper reports, and he'd been out to the house twice to interview the old lady.'

'Could he have had them in the car?' I suggested.

'Shit! I didn't think of that.' She sounded dead tired.

'Look, love, why don't you call it a night and get home. I'll call the police in the morning and see if any notes were found in the car.'

'I can't go home,' she said bitterly. 'You remember how the causeway down the road from the farm used to flood and the council put in their new you-beaut, never-flood-again, cross-my-heart-and-here's-my-hand-on-it-bridge?'

I grinned. 'I remember.'

'Wendy rang me an hour ago,' she said. 'Bloody bridge is a foot under and the water's still rising. She said I'd be better off staying in the city tonight. I don't want to sleep in the flat—I'll go to a motel.'

'No!' I said firmly. 'You come to me, Joss. You can sleep in my bed and I'll have the sofa, and if that's an argument about to start, forget it. I'll come round and get you, so lock up the shop and get ready.'

I hung up on her protests.

Joss and I were—er—friends once, before Bob. Years ago. I couldn't let her go to a friendless, impersonal motel. I fed her and then we had coffee and chunks of Black Forest from the French Patisserie, and she relaxed and began to smile—a little wearily, but better than nothing.

I dozed uneasily on the sofa, weighted down by the drumming rain, but woke with a start at about 1.0 a.m. I lay still, ears straining to catch the small sound that had disturbed me. The rain was no longer pounding the tiles senseless—it was more like a constant whispering overhead. And through it there was something else. A small, choking sound.

Carnie? I thought. Then realized: Joss!

Sliding quietly off the sofa, I felt my way up the stairs to the open mezzanine floor which is my bedroom. The city is never totally dark. Even on the blackest, wettest nights there's still a general glow from the city lights. I could make out the mound of bedclothes which was Joss, buried under a blanket in spite of the oppressive warmth, trying to stifle her sobs with the pillow. I thought about trying to comfort her but I knew she'd reject me, so I went softly back down to the kitchen to make us a pot of tea. In my underpants, but it's nothing Joss hasn't seen before, and she had my dressing-gown.

She went quiet as I snapped the kitchen light on. Carnie, curled up in her basket, opened a sleepy eye, decided there wasn't anything in it for her and cat-napped off again. I took the tea up to Joss who was now sitting up in bed, propped against the pillow.

'Thanks, Micky.' She smiled gratefully and accepted a mug. We drank together in silence.

'Do you want to talk?' I asked after a while.

'Joanna rang earlier.' Bob's wife. 'She told me she was going through Bob's flat first thing in the morning. She's been given his keys and whatever he had with him in the car. She said if she found anything of mine she'd send it to me.'

'Ah!' I watched her. 'A bit abrupt.'

'She was warning me off. Telling me not to go there again. It was just so sudden. I thought I'd have more time to be able to go myself and sort things out. If I'd known, I'd have gone through everything when I was there today. I thought about it, but I couldn't face it so soon.'

'Practical girl, Joanna,' I commented, and she was. Cool, competent, zero feelings. And yet Bob had told me once that, whatever else she was, Joanna was straight as a die.

'And honest,' he'd said. 'She may not always like the truth, but she never shrinks from it.'

'I expect so. But—but—you see, I've really got nothing of Bob's that I could keep. It's a hell of a way to end a relationship. Not even a memento. I'm not the collecting type and it never worried me till now, but I'd like something—a remembrance. Otherwise, other than memories, there's not a lot to show for our time together.'

'Was there anything special you wanted?'

'There was a photograph—us together at a journos' dinner.'

'Joanna might send it with your things,' I comforted her. 'She wouldn't want it herself.'

'Joanna will tear it to shreds,' she said flatly. 'She hated that Bob was happy with me.'

I digested this. 'Tell me about the story he was doing.' I thought it might divert her mind.

She set down her mug and hugged her knees. She was

wearing my pyjama coat and had turned the sleeves back but it was still way too big for her. That and her pale, strained face helped to add to a lost waif look which went straight to my heart. I tried to stop staring at her and listen to what she was telling me.

'He'd done all the articles in the series. He's very keen on the history of the area. He *was*,' she corrected herself bitterly. 'But he was really enthusiastic about this one. He kept saying, "I don't believe what I've got here," and, "This is incredible, if it's true." Stuff like that. I know the place has a pretty weird history. It's supposed to be unlucky or something and the family hasn't had it easy, so maybe it's true.'

'Where is this unlucky place?'

'It's at Bardon, right up on the heights. It's called Darkwater, but don't ask me why, and it's owned by a Mrs Forrest. She's in her seventies and the last of the Darkwater dynasty. I believe there are other family members around but they don't go to Darkwater.'

'I wonder why.' I was interested. 'Maybe it really is unlucky.'

'Maybe they don't get on with Mrs Forrest,' Joss countered. 'Bob said she was a real tartar. He called her the last of the Colonials. Said she was tough as old boots.'

'Does she live there alone?'

'No, she's got a companion. A Mrs Hill. They've been friends all their lives. Went to school together. When Mrs Forrest's husband died, Mrs Hill moved in with her.'

'How old is this place?'

'I think it was built around the 1850s. The bloke who built it, William Forrest, was a very big wig. He was a JP and a founder member of the Queensland Club, and had his own shipping business. The really interesting thing about Darkwater was that it was one of the last homes built by ticket-of-leave men.'

Brisbane doesn't have a pleasant early history. It began as a penal colony and the names of Moreton Bay and Captain Logan were feared and hated even in those brutal times. Convicts who served out their time were given 'tickets of leave', documents which proclaimed they had paid their debt to society and were now free to work. The district was closed as a penal settlement in 1839 and was thrown open to free men, so the few remaining homes built by convicts or ticket-of-leave men are a direct link back to our earliest roots.

'I'll be interested to see this place,' I told Joss. 'I'll make a start in the morning. The sooner I get going, the sooner I can get back to my book.'

'You don't mind really, do you, Micky?' She was slipping lower into the bed and smiled sleepily at me.

'No, love.' I kissed her forehead and collected our mugs. 'I don't mind really.'

I saw Joss off the next morning and carried a protesting Carnie outside to do her duty in the sodden ground. The large, heavy drops from the mango tree striking her fur made her jump and shiver, so I obligingly held the umbrella over her and suffered the drips myself. Al Wang joined us for his T'ai-chi, which he performs gracefully under the mango tree every day, rain or shine. Al lives below me in Flat 3. He's an acupuncturist, philosopher and judo black belt.

'You're bloody mad,' I told him kindly.

'I am waterproof.' He smiled serenely. 'Rain may wet but I am not likely to melt, and it is really quite dry under these thick leaves. This is good, to be in the open air with the smell of the damp earth and to breathe the freshness of the day.'

The humidity was well over 90°. If he breathed too deeply he'd drown! Carnie and I left him to it.

It had occurred to me sometime before the dawn that

if Bob's notes had been with him in the car Joanna would have them now, along with his other possessions. Not a happy thought. Anyone who tangles with Joanna is going to come off second best. I'd need to practise a lot of diplomacy.

The police couldn't recall any papers, but confirmed all Bob's things had been handed over to his wife. Joanna had been feeding her anger for hours by the time I got her on the phone. She'd been to Bob's flat.

'Yes, I remember you, Mr Douglas. You write children's books, I believe.' Polite, but unenthusiastic.

'That's right. We met at a writers' party, years ago. How are you, Joanna?'

'What can I do for you?' I translated this as, 'I have no intention of getting pally, so get on with it.' I got on with it.

'Bob was writing an article about a historical home belonging to a local pioneer family. I've been asked to finish it and I need his notes. He'd been researching the story for days, so it should be about finished. I said I'd tidy up anything and complete it. The notes weren't in his flat, so I wondered if he'd had them with him when he . . . and they'd been passed on to you.'

There was a long, frosty silence, then Joanna said tersely, 'Was this for the *Paddington News?*'

'Er—yes, as a matter of fact, er—' I knew I was beginning to waffle.

'There were no notes,' she said with finality.

'Are you sure, Joanna? No partly written article or notebooks?'

'Mr Douglas, I understand what notes are. There was nothing—and even if there were, I wouldn't be inclined to hand them over to get that bitch out of trouble.'

'Look, Joanna,' I tried again. 'It would be really nice to be able to finish the story. A sort of tribute to Bob. It was the final in a series.'

'I don't give a toss about the series,' she interrupted. 'I've just been finding her little knickknacks all over Bob's flat.' Just as if she hadn't known. This performance of outraged innocence was wasted on me.

'Actually, as Bob was working for the *News*, his notes would belong to the paper. I don't think you have a legal right to them.'

'Well, it's a moot point, isn't it, because as I've already told you, there were no notes.' Her voice was arctic. 'Was there anything else, Mr Douglas?'

In for a penny, in for a pound. 'As a matter of fact, there was,' I said, trying to match her coolth. Some chance! 'I'd very much like to have a photograph Bob had—taken at a journalists' dinner.'

Another long pause while I dithered anxiously at my end of the line.

'A photo of Bob and Miss Paddington News?'

'Yes, that's the one.'

'And you want it for her, do you? A nice little souvenir of her adultery with my husband? Not a hope, Mr Douglas. I mean to burn it, of course.'

'That's not fair, Joanna.' I could be tough, too. 'After all, you've got nothing to blame Joss for. Bob left you well before he met her and it wasn't her fault. At least she made him happy and gave him a chance to stay in journalism, which was his only real love. It might not have been the crime beat but it was still investigative and it was good for him. It saved his life. Joss loved him and knew better than to stifle him. She deserves some memory of their years together. You have everything. His house, his children, all his possessions. She has nothing. Is it going to hurt you to give her one small happy memory back?'

Oops, I thought, I blew it! Bang goes the photo!

Joanna had hung up.

Honestly, I'm an idiot at times. Oh well, if I couldn't get Bob's notes, I'd damned well start from scratch! Read his other articles, match his style. Joss was going to get her story, if it took me the rest of the month. I can be just as stubborn as the next man. Or woman. Sorry, person!

CHAPTER 3

Joss had given me the phone number of Darkwater and I rang Mrs Forrest. The phone was answered by her companion, a gentle-voiced lady who identified herself as Margaret Hill. She sounded shocked to hear of Bob's accident and twittered distressfully into the receiver.

'How *appalling*! Such a *nice* man, so interested in the house and the family. Oh dear, Mr, er, Douglas, did you say? I'm so very, very sorry. And at the bottom of Kaye . . . oh goodness, that's the very spot where Mrs Forrest's own son . . . it's a wicked, steep road and they ought to do something. Oh dear, what a shocking thing to have happened.'

I waited until she drew breath and leaped in. 'I've agreed to take over from Bob and do the article myself.'

'What a *nice* thought. How very good of you. He was so excited to be writing about Darkwater, you know. He made so many notes.'

'Unfortunately, his notes can't be found,' I pursued firmly, 'and I'm going to have to start all over again. Do you think Mrs Forrest would think it an awful intrusion if I asked for another interview?'

'Oh no, no, I'm sure she wouldn't,' the soft voice assured me earnestly. 'She loves to talk about Darkwater. She's so proud of her home and its history. Such a fascinating place, you know.'

'Is she at home now? Can I speak with her, please?'

'Well, sadly, no. She's not as strong as she used to be, although she'd never admit it, and she's resting at the moment.' She brightened. 'But come up anyway, Mr Douglas. I'll show you around and you can stay for afternoon tea and talk to Eileen then. She'll be so sorry to hear about Mr Slater. I'm sure she'll give you all the help she can. What a tragedy! Is that settled, then? You have the address? Good. I'll expect you soon.'

I drove up through the rain along the steep, almost circular terraces that brought me out at the top of Bardon and parked in a narrow side lane which bordered the Darkwater property. Over a tall wooden fence I could see a giant stand of bamboo, rustling and tapping its stems in the rising wind which gusted under my umbrella, showering me with droplets as I turned into Forrest Road and came to the impressive main gate. It was of cast iron, moulded to feature an Australian design of lyrebirds and palm fronds, and was hung from two great stone gateposts, the tops of which were almost invisible among thick, dripping foliage. There was an arch over the gate which carried a Latin motto. I hesitated, suddenly aware of an indefinable feeling of being watched, and looked up and down the street trying to spot the source. Nothing!

I could see a paved driveway beyond the gate leading to the house, which was low-set and screened from curious eyes by a large golden rain tree, suitable for this weather, covered with salmon pink seed pods as delicate as flowers.

Still knowing myself to be under scrutiny, I unlatched the gate, which swung easily open. Turning to close it, I caught a slight movement above me. Two ancient palms flanked the gate and I peered up through the fronds to find my watcher sitting regally on the gatepost like a Siamese statue, sheltered from the wet by the sheer thickness of the greenery and staring back at me enigmatically from brilliant blue, slanted eyes.

I grinned to myself, almost with a sense of relief, and stretched up a hand in friendship. My new acquaintance inclined her neck gracefully and examined my scent with caution. Finally deciding I was harmless, she rubbed her long cream and brown head against my hand, mewed harshly and came head first down the palm tree like a plush cream cascade.

'You're beautiful,' I told her feelingly, 'just gorgeous!'

Obviously bored by such tributes, she briefly rubbed her thick softness around my wet ankles and set off down the driveway towards the house, with another loud call in my direction. The invitation was obvious, and I followed her.

The drive was lined with rose-bushes in full bloom, from great red, velvety, chocolate-box types to crisp yellows, pinks, whites and creams. They'd have made a stunning display but were now a little the worse for wear, their heads bent against the rain, some shedding the odd petal on to the wet grass. But what made me pause with surprise was my first clear view of the house. Darkwater was beautiful! A colonial masterpiece, low-set, with broad sandstone steps leading up to a wide verandah which ran the length of the house and continued around the sides, its iron roof supported by pairs of white columns. The front door was a massive affair of red cedar and on either side four French windows, protected by seven-foot-high louvred shutters of the same timber, gave access to the verandah from the house. I realized that the bushes growing in long beds against the verandah were azaleas and thought how breathtaking the gardens would be later, come spring.

My escort flicked her dark brown tail and trod gracefully up the steps. I followed, noting that the verandah boards were also of red cedar, scarcer than hens' teeth and worth its weight in gold. I stepped reverently to the front door and pulled the old iron bell. I could hear the faint clang as my presence was announced.

After a few moments the great door opened and a woman appeared. She was tall, plump and slightly stooped, with soft white hair, set in somewhat crestfallen waves. Faded blue eyes peered at the world from behind thick spectacles. She smiled a gentle welcome.

'Mr Douglas? How very nice to meet you. I see Su-Lin brought you up. Just leave your umbrella out here. If you open it and set it down it will have a chance to dry out. Oh

dear, isn't this weather tiresome! You look quite damp.
Where did you leave your car? You could have driven right
in, you know.'

I went to speak and she hurried on.

'Call me Margaret, please. Now, come straight through.'

I gazed around as she led me through the entrance hall
into the living-room. It was spacious and high-ceilinged,
furnished with what were obviously the original colonial
chairs, occasional tables, a divan, long-case clock, and stools
covered with petit-point. The room was long and divided
by a great folding cedar door, beautifully carved. A fireplace
big enough to burn quite large logs was set in one wall.

Margaret pointed me to a comfortable leather armchair
and the Siamese, who had followed us in, leaped on to
another to sit, tail twitching slightly, blue eyes watching me
closely.

'We still call this the drawing-room,' Margaret's voice
flowed on. 'It's huge, of course, but we keep the folding door
closed, mostly, and just use this part. It's so much cosier. I
opened it up so you could get the whole effect.'

The room had tall French windows opening on two sides
to the verandah which ran around the house. From the side
windows I could see more beds of roses and azalea bushes
and a graceful jacaranda, through the grey rain gusts.

Margaret plumped herself down opposite me and smiled
expectantly.

'Now, you just ask me anything you want to know,' she
said eagerly. 'I've heard Eileen tell the story of Darkwater
so many times, I know it by heart. I've lived here myself
for sixteen years.'

I took out my notebook. 'Well, I suppose my first question
is, why was the place called Darkwater? It's an unusual
name, isn't it?'

She beamed. 'It is, and that's the first thing everybody
asks. Well, when the original owner, William Forrest, built
here there was a spring—a waterhole. When you looked

into it, the water looked very dark. Something to do with either the minerals in the water or the mosses in the spring. So he called his property Darkwater. There! A simple explanation, isn't it? The water was perfectly drinkable. The spring was converted to a well, and used for many years. Of course, we've been on the town water supply since the 'twenties, when they built the Paddington water tower, but the old well is still out in the garden. All covered over now, but there's a dip in the ground to show where it was.'

'I'd like to see it,' I commented.

'We'll take you all around the garden after tea. What a pity it's still raining. Really, enough is enough.'

'Tell me about William Forrest,' I asked.

'I'll do better than that, I'll show you his portrait.' She got up and I followed. The Siamese yawned widely and came after us.

'Su-Lin?' Margaret sounded surprised. 'She's not usually so companionable.'

'She's a beautiful cat,' I said.

'And she knows it! She's got a twin brother, Mao. He's around somewhere.'

She led me into the next room, which was the dining-room. A long table which accommodated ten straight-backed chairs stood in the centre with a beautiful crystal chandelier overhead. Tall sideboards graced each end of the room and French windows, shuttered at the moment, led, as usual, on to the verandah. The room looked like a show place and, as far as I could see, was stuffed with antique crockery. I had a fleeting impression that the house had been lifted from the nineteenth century and set down, intact, on its commanding hilltop.

Margaret was waiting by the far wall which was hung with portraits. The largest, most imposing, showed a man in his late thirties, with a large moustache, craggy eyebrows and a strong jaw. The most striking feature was his eyes. The artist had caught the stern, unyielding expression which

was highlighted by dark, piercing eyes like an eagle's, deep
set under those bristling brows.

'A strong face,' I said, impressed.

'He was a strong man,' Margaret said, 'and stubborn.
He let nothing stand in his way. You'll see that face again
and again in his descendants and his character, his strong
will and dominant personality, comes out from time to time
in the Forrests. A great family, Mr Douglas.'

'I take it Mrs Forrest is not a direct descendant, but a
Forrest by marriage,' I said thoughtfully.

'Oh heavens, no! Whatever made you think . . .? Oh,
the name, of course. No, Eileen is a direct descendant of
William and Amelia Forrest. She was married to Clifford
Trent, and then she was Eileen Forrest-Trent. But when
poor Clifford—so tragic—she won't speak of it, even now,
you know—well, let's just say when he died, she reverted
back to just the Forrest. Didn't want to be reminded. Poor
Eileen.'

'What happened to him?' I asked, interested.

'No, I can't tell you. She won't have it mentioned. I'm
sorry.' Her gentle mouth shut like a steel trap and she
seemed determined not to say any more. I returned to
William's portrait. He struck me as a man with a purpose
who would probably stop at nothing to get his own way. It
was painted in every line of his face. A dangerous man to
cross, my inner voice said.

'I had my pen at the ready. 'Tell me about him, Margaret.'

'Well, he was English, of course, like so many pioneers.
His family was from Kent. He was an adventuresome boy
and came out to seek his fortune in the new land when he
was only fifteen. He made a name for himself in Sydney.
He was an astute businessman and he already had quite a
sizeable fortune when he came to Brisbane—Moreton Bay,
the colony was, of course. He arrived here in 1849, ten years
after the penal settlement had been closed. Being William,

he lost no time in establishing himself and four years later was a very prominent citizen. He liked the Ashgrove Hills and decided to build here in 1853. There was a wonderful view across the town and all the prominent citizens were picking the best of the hill country around Brisbane.'

'I was told the house was built by ex-convicts.'

She nodded. 'Ticket-of-leave men, that's right. We're a last link with the convict days here. The last of the wild colonial boys. And they were wild.' She laughed suddenly. 'Do you know, they had running battles with the aborigines and on nights when balls were held here, they had to have armed guards patrolling the grounds to discourage the blacks.'

My imagination could see it clearly, in this gracious old dining-room. The ladies in their ball dresses, elegant gentlemen, civilians and officers, servants laden with heavy silver serving dishes, the crystal chandelier making the glasses sparkle, the polite conversation and, outside, the wild Australian bush close around them and the sounds of armed men patrolling, perhaps watched by the sullen dark eyes of the original owners of the land who resented this invasion of the white folk.

Margaret's voice recalled me. 'Now *this* is Margaret Jane Forrest.' The face was that of a pretty woman, perhaps in her mid-twenties, with a lace shawl about her white shoulders and her hair in dark ringlets. 'She was William's first wife,' Margaret went on. 'You know, I'm glad that she and I have the same name. It makes me feel almost part of the Family. Margaret and William married in 1854 but sadly, she died in childbirth only a year later. It was very hard in those days. Well, there was only a riding track up to the hills and the midwife didn't arrive in time. Poor William was devastated. He adored Margaret. She was the daughter of another prominent businessman. Very well-to-do. She had a fortune in her own right, so her death made William immensely wealthy. Not that he cared about that.

He shut himself away, left his business in the hands of his manager and lived in seclusion for a year with his baby son, William Junior. Such a sad story.'

Sad, but fairly common. Our pioneers had to be tough to survive the hard conditions, the many tropical diseases and the primitive medical knowledge.

'But he did remarry?' I asked.

'My word, he did! He realized eventually that he needed to provide a mother for poor orphaned William and he wanted to establish a family. He began to re-enter society and eventually married Amelia. That was in 1857.' I jotted down the names and dates and followed my guide. She had moved on to the next portrait. Here was a severe-looking woman with a prominent nose and smooth dark hair plaited around her head. A large cameo brooch was pinned at her throat. She looked a good match for the strong William.

'Amelia was a widow. Her husband had been a colonel in the army and had died three years earlier of one of those "colonial fevers" you hear so much about.'

I looked carefully at Amelia and thought I could detect a softness in the eyes and mouth which was overshadowed by her stern face and that nose.

'I don't believe it does her justice,' Margaret said sadly. 'Eileen has a miniature of Amelia and she really looks quite pretty. It wasn't a love match, but she was a good wife and mother and I believe they grew very close. She bore William ten children. Of the eleven Forrest children, only four survived. Do you know,' she dropped her voice confidingly, 'the poor Forrest family seems to have been positively *dogged* with bad luck from the time William built Darkwater. I know there were a lot of premature deaths in those days, but there were so many odd *accidents* as well. I'd never let Eileen hear me say it, but I sometimes wonder . . .'

I must say I wondered a little, too. Hard times they were, but four out of eleven didn't seem like a very good average.

However, what Margaret wondered I never found out. We were both startled by a stern voice behind us.

'Who is this man, Margaret, and what is he doing here?'

CHAPTER 4

I watched Eileen Forrest with interest as Margaret's twittering explanations ran on. She was not more than five feet five inches tall, and thin to the point of frailness. She carried herself rigidly erect, leaning almost imperceptibly on an ebony cane. You couldn't have found a greater contrast to her tall, robust, stooping friend. She wore a long dark dress with a high collar and at her throat was pinned—my eyes flashed back to the portrait—Amelia's cameo. Her hair was smooth dark steel, and plaited around her head exactly as Amelia's, but her piercing dark eyes and strong jaw echoed William. She was undoubtedly a descendant of William and Amelia Forrest.

She spoke with an English inflection and almost no trace of an Australian accent, as so many of her generation did, thinking the 'ocker' accent common. Her words were precise and clipped. She turned her eyes to me and I felt the immense power of her personality.

'A car accident?' she repeated. 'How very tragic. So you are to continue where Mr Slater left off. Were you a great friend of Mr Slater's, Mr Douglas?'

'I knew him,' I countered carefully. I felt she was attending too closely to every word. 'I'm a friend of the lady who runs the *Paddington News*. It's for her I'm doing the story—with your permission, of course.'

'Miss Joss Bates, yes.' She nodded. Her gaze wasn't exactly unwelcoming, but—I cast around for a word—guarded, that was it. There was a definite tension in the air which was suddenly broken by Su-Lin, who gave her strident miaow and arched around my legs, then rubbed her face against my shoes.

Mrs Forrest looked sharply at me. 'Well!' she exclaimed. 'She's never done that before!'

Margaret laughed encouragingly. 'Oh, she's taken a real fancy to Mr Douglas. She brought him up from the gate and hasn't let him out of her sight. She followed him in here.'

'I see.' She walked towards me with slow, firm steps. 'Do you believe cats are psychic, Mr Douglas?'

'Sometimes, maybe,' I said. 'They certainly seem so.'

'You are a cat person?'

'Well, I have an Abyssinian flatmate, Carnation Belle Douglas.'

'A rare cat, the Abyssinian. I have two Siamese myself. I see Margaret has been giving you the family history.'

She released me at last from her uncomfortably close scrutiny and turned towards the portraits. Presumably, being Su-Lin's new friend, I was acceptable.

'I'm overwhelmed by this beautiful house,' I told her. She softened perceptibly.

'It is a very rare place, Darkwater. I have always striven to maintain it exactly as William and Amelia would have wished, and I believe they would scarcely notice any difference, were they to return here.'

'We were talking about Amelia,' Margaret broke in eagerly, 'and the sad loss of her children.'

'Such deaths were common occurrences,' Mrs Forrest said tartly. 'Many families suffered similar losses. There was fever, smallpox, tuberculosis, and then, bright, adventurous children will always find trouble.'

'Can you tell me something about the children?' I asked.

She looked for a moment as if she was going to refuse, then changed her mind.

'If I seem reluctant, Mr Douglas, it is because there has been a lot of nonsense talked about Darkwater being unlucky and the many deaths offered as proof.' Her stern look wilted the garrulous Margaret, who had fallen strangely silent. 'Many women, for instance, died in childbirth as Margaret Jane did, and nothing can be read into that. It was a condition of those hard times. Of Amelia's children, her two firstborn girls were taken by smallpox in 1860, but many children were, you know, and it was not at all unusual. A couple of years later one of the boys was playing with his father's gun, as boys will, and it discharged, killing him instantly. There was also a riding accident. William Junior and his two half-brothers, Adrian and John, who were then aged nine and seven, were riding into town when something frightened the horses and they bolted, killing John. Again, riding accidents were common enough.'

I looked up from my notes. 'Was it ever known what scared the horses?'

'Not definitely. Both surviving boys were shocked by the accident. From old diaries, it seems William said a wild aboriginal man stepped out of the bush and shook his spear.' Her face tightened suddenly. 'You realize that in those days the hills were still in their natural, wild bush state.' I nodded. 'Adrian maintained that it was a snake which crossed the track and that there was no aboriginal. You know how it is with eyewitness accounts, and with two badly frightened boys! I believe it was a snake. After all, by 1860 the North Brisbane native tribes were virtually extinct. William probably saw a bush moving or a tree branch from the corner of his eye and imagined the rest.'

'That's very likely,' I agreed. After all, it was her story and she ought to know, but what had disturbed her?

'Eileen has some charming miniatures of the children.' Margaret was back in the conversation. 'Do show him, Eileen dear.'

Mrs Forrest responded with an inclination of her head and opened a sideboard drawer. Inside, laid in rows on dark green velvet, were several miniatures. She set them gently, one by one, on the dining table. I wanted to pick them up but hesitated, feeling a steely gaze on me. I contented myself by bending to examine them where they were and received a nod of approval. It might well be a museum.

'The young girls who died of smallpox were not painted, and there were stillborn twins,' Mrs Forrest said, 'but here are Adrian and John—' the portrait showed two fair-haired boys, frozen with typical Victorian stiffness—'and a later one of Adrian.' The same solemn face three or four years older; a boy moving swiftly into manhood but with a gentle face and rather dreamy expression, obviously a throwback to some gentleness in Amelia. 'Here is Amelia-Jane. She died at fourteen. This was painted a year before. She was always a sickly girl. She contracted tuberculosis.' The pale face showed her mother's gentle eyes and prominent nose. Mrs Forrest passed her over quickly as if frailty in a Forrest was not something to be discussed in public.

'Now, this is William Junior.' There was a hint of pride in her voice. He was a chip off the old block if I ever saw one. A young child maybe, but the face already showed the same stern gaze and piercing eyes of the older William. Those eyes wouldn't miss much! I shivered suddenly, looking at that arrogant lift of the head. Darkwater's crown prince.

The final miniatures were of another boy, Andrew, who had the strong, stern Forrest face, two girls, Charlotte and Mary, and two further portraits of William Junior, who was painted at various stages of his growth but, to my mind, with no improvement.

We examined the rest of the large portraits which showed the only children to have made it to adulthood, and their families.

'What happened to them?' I asked as Mrs Forrest, Su-Lin and I walked slowly through the house. The central passage branched and we turned to the left. The house was divided into two wings. Margaret had left us to make the afternoon tea.

'Mary married the eldest son of an old English family in 1887, when she was twenty-one. He was out here visiting friends. They returned to England. Mary never came back to Australia. Andrew married a local girl and settled down at Darkwater. He was my grandfather. Charlotte never married but stayed on at Darkwater with Andrew and his wife. She was a great champion of women's causes and became headmistress of a girls' school. Adrian left Darkwater and moved to Western Queensland, where he bought a sheep station. He married a country girl and fathered a large family but severed all ties with the Darkwater Forrests. He never really belonged here.' She sounded disapproving, and I was about to query her statement when she opened a door and said, reverently:

'This is William's study.'

I entered with curiosity. She'd said 'is', not 'was', and with good reason. A large portrait of the senior Forrest hung over the fireplace, dominating the room. It was of a much older William than the painting in the dining-room; a man in his late fifties. The artist had caught the tremendous energy of the man, and his personality was so strong in every corner of this malest of male domains that I could believe he'd just stepped out for some business matter and would be back at any moment. His ornate and highly polished oak desk held his pipe and silver tobacco box, his guns adorned one wall, his riding whip was tossed on a chair as if he'd just thrown it there. A small picture of Amelia with two of the young girls stood in a silver frame on the desk and a portrait of young William had pride of place on the wall opposite the desk, so the father could look up at his son while he worked. Maybe it was just the heavy, close atmosphere but I couldn't explain the eerie feeling that made my hackles rise.

'It has always been kept as William liked it, and no one else has used it,' Mrs Forrest was saying. 'It is a point of honour with the Forrests to remember William and keep his house strong.'

There didn't seem to be anything to say. I preserved what I hoped would look like an awed silence and tried to pin down the cause of my discomfort. I had a strong suspicion that if I'd known William Forrest I'd have disliked him. The museum-like-room depressed me and the steady rain with its interminable splattering on the verandah's iron roof did nothing to ease my mind.

'Amelia's room is across the hall.' Mrs Forrest broke the silence. 'We'll just take a quick look. She liked to be near William and worked there when he was in his study.'

I followed her out of William's preserve with relief and was soothed by Amelia's room with its embroidery box inlaid with ivory, the tapestry firescreen and matching chair covers in blue with pink and yellow rosebuds and the face screen which preserved Amelia's delicate complexion as she sat by the fire.

More portraits on the walls—mostly of the children. These Forrests must have been a boon for the local artists.

Su-Lin yowled suddenly and looked fixedly at the door. I jumped, my heart suddenly racing.

'Margaret must be ready for us,' Mrs Forrest said. 'Come along, Mr Douglas, I can show you the rest of the house after tea.'

CHAPTER 5

'When William decided to build in the Ashgrove Hills, he purchased sixteen acres for the sum of sixteen pounds ten shillings.'

We were drinking coffee in the drawing-room; poured from a nineteenth-century silver coffee pot and served in fine bone china cups. All very elegant. Mrs Forrest drank from an exquisite Chinese patterned cup. 'It belonged to the first William,' she'd explained quietly as I admired the ancient pattern. 'I always use it.'

The coffee was excellent; strong, with an unusual taste and an underlying bitterness which, curiously, didn't detract from its pleasant flavour.

'We blend our own,' Mrs Forrest explained. 'The difference is the Turkish we mix with it. It's the same recipe William used. We never use that instant rubbish. Darkwater coffee is an acquired taste, but once acquired, our visitors enjoy it very much.'

'As I'm doing,' I told her. 'Yes, please, I'd love another cup.'

Margaret had put on quite a spread with dainty sandwiches, fairy cakes, lamingtons so light they'd melt in your mouth and homemade shortbread. Eileen Forrest had taken me back to the founding of Darkwater, and spoke with an obvious passion for her subject.

'William was a very influential man,' she continued. 'He had his own shipping company and several stores and he worked tirelessly for the cause to make the district a separate colony from New South Wales. He was among the first to begin moves for separation. Of course, there was great opposition from the Government in Sydney. They could see themselves losing a very rich colony indeed. Perhaps you'd like to see what was written in the *Sydney Herald* of the day?'

She passed me a clipping from a folder she'd brought with her.

'I kept some of these articles out for Mr Slater,' she explained, and watched with cool amusement as I read:

> It is difficult to mete out the portions of laughter, pity and contempt which must be awarded to our misguided fellow-colonists lying to the northward of the thirtieth degree of latitude.

You have to laugh. Mind you, a lot of New South Welshmen still feel the same way and heap scorn on us Banana Benders. We don't mind. When you live in Paradise, you recognize jealousy when you hear it.

'There was a very powerful lobby in the south, as you can imagine,' Mrs Forrest went on, 'but, in spite of everything, the new colony of Queensland was proclaimed on Separation Day, on the 10th of December in 1859. William writes a glowing account of the day in his diary. He was as proud as a peacock! The proclamation was made from the first floor balcony of the Deanery, which of course was Government House in those days, and the Government Resident for New South Wales, Captain Wickham, was replaced by our first Governor, Sir George Ferguson Bowen. It was a gala day, with all the ladies in their very best dresses and bonnets, the military men in their uniforms and the civilians dressed to the nines. Amelia bought a new hat for the occasion.'

She sounded as if she'd been there and once again I felt an odd distaste, in spite of my interest. Margaret was listening, leaning forward avidly. I could imagine the bright, summer scene 150 years ago, and hoped they had better weather for it than we were having now.

'Would it be possible to see the grounds?' I ventured. 'I

know it's still raining, but Margaret said you might show me around after tea.'

'If we were going to let the rain stop us, we'd never get anything done these days,' Mrs Forrest said drily. 'Come on, Mr Douglas, if you're finished.'

I had. I thanked Margaret for the food.

'Oh, Mr Douglas, it was a real pleasure.' She smiled delightedly. 'So nice to be able to feed a man with a hearty appetite.'

'Call me Micky,' I told both the ladies. 'Most people do.'

'Well, all right, Micky, I will,' Margaret hesitated, looking at the empty cups and plates as if torn between clearing away and coming with us.

'Oh, do come along if you want to, Margaret!' Mrs Forrest made the decision for her. 'This way, Mr Douglas.'

'Right!' We processed through the hall, Mrs Forrest in the lead, Su-Lin and me walking together and Margaret bringing up the rear.

The ladies paused to pick their umbrellas out of the hallstand, and put on their coats which hung next to it. Mrs Forrest took a pair of garden gloves from her coat pocket and slipped them on. We went out on to the wide front verandah. The rain had dropped to a depressing drizzle as we set out down the front steps and around the side of the house.

'The roses are wonderful,' I commented.

'Oh yes, quite spectacular, although sadly spoiled by the weather. The Darkwater roses are famous, locally. They win quite a lot of prizes in the shows.'

What else! Everything at Darkwater was class.

I felt more comfortable out of the house and cheerfully followed Mrs Forrest as she showed off the gardens, pausing every now and then to nip off a dead flower here, a leaf there.

'Originally, of course, the grounds were very much more extensive,' she went on, 'and William had them landscaped.

He was rather scornful of the local flora, unfortunately, as were most of our pioneers.' My ears pricked up. A criticism of William? Surely not! 'However, you can understand their attitude with everything they saw so very different from what they were used to in Europe.' Aha! Mitigating circumstances! 'They thought the Australian wild flowers uninteresting, even dull. They tended to plant European gardens, although the climate was usually so unsuitable.' She swept a hand towards the rose-beds. 'William actually imported the roses and azaleas from England. He paid two thousand pounds, which was a huge sum in those days, and many of these are the original plants. The azaleas are wonderful in the spring. Just a riot of colour. William was interested in botany, by the way, and later came to appreciate the Australian plants.'

She paused beside a magnificent bunya pine tree, a giant towering above us. 'William planted this very tree,' she said warmly. We had a moment's silence. 'There was an avenue of pines, but this is the only one left. Little by little the land was sold as the suburb grew and now we have only the land you see here,' she finished sadly. It seemed a large area to me, but I tried to look suitably grieved.

We walked past a row of travellers' palms holding their fans to screen a side garden. Across the hills the white walls and tower of Fernberg, the Governor's house, could be clearly seen, as well as the water tower and, to the right, the high rises of the city, standing grey and ghostly in the misty rain.

'This was William and Amelia's favourite garden. Their pride and joy.' Mrs Forrest had stopped with me. Margaret was trying to shelter Su-Lin and getting very wet herself. 'They enjoyed a magnificent view across town, as you see, and all the surrounding countryside. Of course, Fernberg wasn't built until 1865 so they saw only the hills and bush land.' She stopped impatiently.

'Margaret, you're dripping all over Su-Lin. Do go in and

take her with you. And you'd better dry yourself. You're
quite wet.'

Margaret gave us a sheepish smile and began to retrace
her steps, calling Su-Lin who went with her, after a back-
ward glance at me.

Mrs Forrest gave me that sharp look and continued to
walk, picking her way carefully across the wet grass.

As we rounded the corner, I could just see through the
greyness the TV towers on Mount Coot-tha and Stuart-
holme Convent perched on its eyrie, high above the surrounding hills. The land at the back of the house stretched
out like a plateau and was bordered by a thick hedge. I
walked towards it but Mrs Forrest recalled me sternly.

'There's nothing to see there. The land plunges down
quite steeply into a natural bush area. Just rocks and scrub
and a few wild native tobacco plants.'

I paused and looked back at her. She was looking definitely bothered.

'Is it part of your land?'

'Oh yes, it all belongs to Darkwater, but it's quite inac-
cessible. There used to be a track down but it was never
safe so it was allowed to grow over. Children will explore,
so William had Andrew, my father, build a fence to keep
youngsters out of harm's way. Then he grew the hedges for
extra security.' Her voice took on an impatient tone. 'Do
come away, it's dangerous.'

I wondered how dangerous it could be, with a fence and
an impenetrable hedge, but returned obediently to her side.
She quickly turned her back on the drop and continued the
tour of the grounds, but suddenly a tremor ran through me.
I frowned, trying to analyse my odd mood, and realized
Mrs Forrest was still speaking. 'Over here was the kitchen,'
she said, and smiled slightly at my surprised look. 'Oh yes,
most of the original colonial homes had separate kitchens.
It reduced the danger of fire from wood stoves and restricted
the servants' and labourers' entry into the main house. The

servants had their own quarters at the back. We'll go back that way and you can see. The kitchen was a large building with a great stone-flagged floor and a huge baker's oven.'

We began to walk back towards the house.

'Look here.' Mrs Forrest bent and picked up a fragment of brick and handed it to me. I looked inquiringly at her.

'The bricks were made on site for the ovens and fireplaces. There was a kiln here. The timber was all dressed and prepared up here and the shingles for the roof as well. They were once all split wood but the roof was re-covered with corrugated iron before I was born. Now here are the servants' quarters.'

The house was higher at the back as the land dropped several feet from the front. It was set firmly on a wall built from blocks of sandstone. Small, high grilles were set at intervals along the top of the wall.

We entered through a low wooden door which she unlocked with a key she'd taken out of her pocket. The servants' rooms were small and dark, with the only light filtering in from the narrow grilles I'd noticed. The whole area struck chill and musty. There was little furniture here, only a couple of old iron bed frames, various sealed wooden tea chests, and the odd rickety chest and table. We went from room to room down a narrow, dark passageway.

'They're not used now, of course, except for storage and—' Mrs Forrest pointed to a pile of soft woollen rags in a corner of one of the rooms—'Su-Lin and her brother Mao like to sleep down here for some reason, and you know when cats take a fancy to a place . . .' She left the sentence unfinished and I grinned sympathetically. Yes, I did know.

'Are you sure only the cats come here?' I asked. As well as the stored boxes there was an old mattress on the floor and a familiar scent in the air.

'Of course.' She spoke emphatically with a sideways glance at me. 'No one else has access. The door is kept locked and the cats come down by the servants' stairs in the

house. This way.' She went out of the room and I turned
to follow her but from the corner of my eye a movement
made me spin around. I gave a startled exclamation and
she looked back.

'Whatever is the matter, Mr Douglas?' she asked tartly.

'I could have sworn . . .' I hesitated, not wishing to alarm
two elderly ladies living on their own, but: 'I thought I saw
a snake,' I said uncertainly.

'A snake?' She looked her disbelief.

'Well . . .' Again I hesitated. Now I wasn't sure. 'I
thought it came from behind the mattress and disappeared
down there.' I pointed to a crack where the great stone
blocks met the floor. Far too small a space. I felt like a
complete fool, and I'd certainly upset my hostess. Her face
set.

'Really, Mr Douglas, that's not very likely. There have
been no snakes at Darkwater for many years and I can't see
one taking up residence with two very efficient hunting cats,
can you?'

I supposed not, and I saw only the briefest movement,
but my mind retained the impression of a dark-banded
snake a foot or so in length. However, there was certainly
nothing there now. I assumed I'd been wrong and followed
her out of the room and up the stone servants' stairs to the
back of the house.

'Now if there's anything more you need, you must certainly telephone and ask.' Mrs Forrest was clearly indicating
my time was up. 'You should have quite a lot for a nice
article about William and Amelia and, now you've seen the
house, it will make a good background for your story.' I had
been dismissed.

Margaret Hill was nowhere in sight as I farewelled Mrs
Forrest. She asked me to send her a copy of the article and
closed the door as I stepped off the verandah. Half way
down the rose-bordered drive I looked back to the house.
Su-Lin and her double, presumably the elusive Mao, were

sitting on either side of the steps watching me fixedly from behind a steady curtain of drops running off the edge of the verandah roof. Again I felt an odd shiver and was strangely relieved to close the gate behind me.

As I started the Capri I realized that I hadn't seen the well which had given Darkwater its name. Perhaps another time . . .

CHAPTER 6

I headed back through the wet streets towards Paddington. Through the steady rain I could see the weathered concrete water tower high above the suburb, and then the white walls of Government House through the trees. Bob had driven this way two nights ago and had turned into the roundabout at the top of Kaye Street as he must have done practically every day, heading for his flat at Torwood.

Obeying an impulse, I blinkered right and followed the roundabout. It certainly wasn't a secret that Kaye Street needed watching. Signs proclaimed the danger, warning trucks to change to low gear and the international car out of control on skid marks sign clearly reminded motorists that Kaye Street was slippery when wet. I took heed and eased down through the rain gusts. Half way along, a black curve line of burnt rubber slewed across the road. I winced and continued down, pulling up at the bottom.

The site of the accident was evident. The Governor had a nasty tear in his wire fence, a tree standing too close was missing a quantity of bark and there was a scattering of windscreen glass. I stood under my umbrella with my head bent. Poor Bob. But *why*? I recalled that black skid mark. Slashing from the right side across to the left. Bob must have been coming down on the wrong side of the road and perhaps encountered another motorist coming up which caused him to swerve violently back to his side, throwing the car out of control. But Bob was very familiar with the street and its hazards and must have known, unless . . . I pushed the unwelcome thought away but it persisted, nagging at the back of my mind. What if Bob had been drinking? I know he'd sworn off the grog years ago, but just supposing he'd started again, unbeknown to Joss? How else could I account for him high-tailing it down Kaye Street on a wet night, on the wrong side of the road?

He'd been coming back from Darkwater, according to Joss. Presumably Mrs Forrest or Margaret would have noticed if he'd been drunk, or at least not in full control. The police would certainly know. It would have been the first thing they'd checked at the autopsy, the amount of alcohol in the bloodstream.

A car drove slowly down in low gear, the driver peering through the rain which was changing from steady to bloody uncomfortable. He looked curiously at me as he passed, probably wondering who the fool was standing in the downpour talking to himself. I squelched back to the Capri and, with a last look at that eloquent break in the fence, climbed into the comparative dry—except I'd brought a ton of water back with me.

I turned the car around and headed back up Kaye Street deep in thought. Margaret Hill had let slip that Mrs Forrest's son had come to some sort of grief in this very place. Nasty!

Carnie went over my trouser legs with rapt attention, eyes half closed, mouth slightly open to get the full scent.

'She was Siamese,' I said, 'and made quite a play for me as well. Nice little thing. Blue eyes.'

Carnie turned her back and began deliberately to wash herself.

It was growing dark when the phone rang. Joss sounded troubled.

'Can I stay the night again?' she asked. 'I don't want to be a nuisance but our bloody safe-as-houses, last-a-lifetime, no-more-worries bridge has been wrecked. A tree came down in the flood and damaged the supports, so even if it wasn't two feet under I couldn't get home.'

'I've got a casserole in the oven, waiting,' I assured her. 'Stop at the tavern on the way and get us a bottle.'

A subdued Joss arrived half an hour later with a roll of what looked like blotting paper under one arm. She handed over the wine, pulled her wet boots off and collapsed on the sofa.

'I feel bloody,' she observed. 'Micky, are you busy with the food, or can we talk?'

'Fire away!' I poured us a glass of wine. She looked as if she needed it and I wasn't feeling the brightest. I sat down opposite her. Carnie, still offended with me, joined Joss and draped artistically over her lap.

'Did you go to Darkwater?' Joss asked the question a little anxiously, watching me over the rim of her glass.

'Yes, I made the pilgrimage.' She looked an inquiry. 'The whole damned place is a shrine to the original owners, William and Amelia Forrest,' I explained. 'I'm beginning to think the present Mrs Forrest is a bit of a nutter. She's got the whole place preserved as the Forrests left it and she speaks of them almost as if they were still around. She's like an encyclopædia on the subject of Darkwater. Knows every detail of the family going back generations. Mind you,' I added, 'it's a wonderful place. It must have been magnificent in its day. Coach house, stables, separate kitchen—all gone now, of course. And the whole place is full of red cedar. You should just see the folding door that divides what they call the drawing-room. Cedar, intricately carved. It's a museum piece. God knows what the place would fetch on the market. A fortune, I should think. It's even got the original servants' quarters.'

She had remained silent, just watching me. I said gently, 'I'm a little puzzled why Bob got so excited, love. It's a marvellous house and an interesting history but nothing you couldn't match with any of the other really old dynasties, I should think.'

Joss sat brooding for a minute, then slowly reached for the roll of paper she'd dropped on the sofa when she'd arrived.

'Bob always had a desk blotter—one of those big squares with a leather back. He didn't use a fountain pen or work with ink but he liked to have it to doodle on. It helped him think.' She unrolled the paper. 'I was cleaning out his desk and I noticed this. He'd just put a fresh sheet in so it was nearly blank. He'd usually have it just covered in messages and drawings. Look.' She thrust the sheet at me. In one corner, in Bob's neat ballpoint, was the word 'Deathwater' and, in a circle of inward pointing arrows, was a question:

'How did William really die?'

I looked up at Joss. '*Deathwater?*' I said. She shrugged. I read the words again, then noticed a name, John Curtis, and a 366 telephone number in the opposite corner.

'Is this anything to do with the other?' I pointed to the name.

She frowned, thinking. 'There's a John Curtis who comes in to look up back issues of the *News* from time to time. He's interested in local history. He was probably giving Bob some info on the series.'

'366 is Ashgrove,' I mused. 'I'll give him a ring and see if he knows anything about Darkwater.'

'Why Deathwater?' Joss asked. 'Presumably he's talking about Darkwater, isn't he?'

'Looks that way,' I agreed.

'And the reference to William. Does he mean the William Forrest who built Darkwater?'

'Well, there were two that I know of,' I told her. 'William the founder and his son, William Jr.'

'How did they die, then?'

'Joss, I don't know.' I thought back. 'Mrs Forrest gave me so much of the history but she didn't seem to like speaking of any of the deaths in the family. She said people used them to label the place as unlucky. But, as she pointed out, premature deaths were a way of life a hundred and thirty years ago. Stillborn kids, tropical diseases, TB, things like that; and accidents. No, she didn't say how either of the Williams died and I didn't think to ask her. There was too much to get in one session, anyway.'

'Can you go back?' Joss was speaking with a queer intensity.

'Do you think it's important? For the article, I mean. I've got enough already to do quite a story.'

'*Bob* thought it was important,' Joss insisted. 'Something got him all worked up. Something made him go on looking after *he'd* got plenty of material already. He was . . .' She hesitated. 'I was almost going to say, on a crusade. Just like when he used to be on the crime stories. He had a nose for crime. He must have stumbled on something that excited him and this is the only clue we have. See those arrows?' She pointed. 'He's gone over and over them, round and round the circle. He did that when he was really wrestling with a problem.'

'What do you think?' I asked.

'I think that *he* thought that one of your William Forrests died in some way that didn't add up. He'd have spotted anything like that, any discrepancy.'

I considered her statement. 'I think that should be "Williams Forrest",' I said. 'And what if it were true? That was a hundred years ago. It might have been of interest to Bob but I can't see that it has any relevance, really. I can't put it in the story, there'd be absolutely no way of proving such a thing. Anyway, how on earth could I find out?'

Joss had a little worried expression.

'I think . . .' she began, and looked at me, conscience-stricken. 'I think the casserole's burning.'

CHAPTER 7

I managed to salvage enough dinner for us and we finished the bottle Joss had brought. The rain thundered on the roof making communication difficult, so we sat close to hear each other while I told her all about Darkwater.

'I wasn't shown all the rooms, but it's a huge place. Margaret Hill probably does the cooking, but I can't see those two keeping such a place in order—and certainly not doing all that gardening. The grounds are immaculate.'

'They'll have help,' Joss guessed. 'Probably hire a gardener and a housekeeper or a maid of some kind to do the housework.'

'I'd have liked to find out more about Mrs Forrest. Bob was right about her. She's a tyrant. Dresses to look like Amelia Forrest, William's second wife, and has William's features. Before she joined us, Margaret told me something interesting. She said William's traits come out from time to time in the Forrests. Described him as strong, stubborn and ruthless with a dominating personality. I can tell you, his face does nothing to deny it. I wouldn't have liked to cross swords with old William. And I'll bet Mrs Forrest has inherited his character. My instinct was to tread very softly around her.'

'Didn't she tell you anything about herself?'

'Not a word, except a reference to the stables still being there in her childhood. And apparently her husband died in some nasty way—well, that was the impression I got from Margaret, who rattled on indiscriminately. Now *she'd* not be able to hide anything.'

'Was his name William?' Joss pounced.

'No, hang on a minute.' I took out my notebook. 'A Clifford Trent. It came up because I thought, seeing as she called herself Forrest, she must have married into the family, but she was Mrs Trent. Pardon me, Mrs *Forrest*-Trent. Didn't even drop the Forrest when she married and as soon as good old Cliff kicks the bucket, she drops his name like a hot potato. Margaret said his death was tragic and said Mrs Forrest never spoke of it. When I asked her what happened to him, she shut up like a clam.'

'Interesting,' Joss commented. 'Easy enough to find out, though. The newspapers of the time; and you could talk to the neighbours, find out what he did and how he died.'

I was horrified. 'Joss, I can't do that. It's none of our business. After all, if Mrs Forrest doesn't want it talked about . . .'

She sighed impatiently. 'Micky, you'll never make a reporter. Don't you feel even vaguely curious?'

I had to admit it. 'And especially about one thing,' I remembered. 'One of William the founder's sons, Adrian, was quite different in features, temperament—you could see it in his face. A gentle, open face, dreamy expression. Nice-looking kid. Now it was he who left Darkwater, severed all ties with the place and set himself up on a sheep station out west. And Mrs Forrest made an odd remark. She said he never really belonged at Darkwater. She sounded scornful, as if he'd been found lacking in true Forrest family spirit, but I'd have had a lot more time for Adrian than the other Forrests. Young William was a dead ringer for his dad and had a nasty, supercilious look about him. Of them all, Adrian got my vote as the Forrest most likely to have a spark of decent human feeling.'

'Are you going to follow up on Mrs Forrest, then?' Joss demanded. 'You'll need a bit about her for the article and you could ask about the two Williams at the same time.'

'Ye—es,' I said slowly. 'I got the feeling she'd given me all she was going to. She dismissed me like royalty. She did say I could telephone and ask if I wanted any more info, but she implied with the same breath that it shouldn't be necessary and she certainly didn't suggest I visit again, which is a pity because I had the oddest yen to see the old well.' I'd told Joss how the house had come by its name.

'Why don't you ring and pump Margaret Hill if she's the gabby one?' she suggested. I winced. Sometimes Joss is almost too direct. But it was a good idea, none the less.

'I'll think about it,' I promised. 'I'll ring this bloke Curtis and see what he can tell me.' I didn't add that I'd also ring the police to see if Bob had been drunk that night. No point in upsetting Joss needlessly.

'I'll have to wash my undies and dry them. I've no clothes,' Joss said. 'My jeans will do another day, but can I borrow a shirt?' She picked up my robe and headed for the bathroom.

It was a nice feeling to have Joss washing her dainties in my bathroom basin again. They'd be dripping on the shower curtain rail over the bath when I was ready for my shower. And afterwards we'd have coffee and supper and listen to music, arguing the merits of classical and country, and after that . . . I pulled myself back with a jerk and pushed the thought away. After that, Joss would go to my bed and I would go to the sofa and we would sleep, separate and chaste. She certainly didn't need the other right now.

Joss appeared, clean and damp-haired, as I finished the washing up. She leaned against the fridge door and watched me, again with that troubled look. I wished with all my heart that I could kiss it and make it better but Joss is a big girl now and she knows it doesn't work that way.

I gave her a rallying smile instead and she perched on the divider.

'Bob's funeral is on Friday.' That was in two days. 'There was a notice in the paper.'

'Are you going?' I wished she wouldn't but knew she would.

'I'd like to. To say goodbye properly. Joanna will be

there, of course, and she'll be furious, but I want to go, Micky.'

'Need an escort?'

'Would you come with me? Oh Micky.'

'Of course, love. No one can stop you going to a funeral, not that I've heard, anyway. We'll go and brave Joanna together.'

'Thanks.' She threw me a grateful look. 'You go and have your shower and I'll brew us some coffee.'

The next day I typed up what I had of the Darkwater story, copying Bob's style as best I could. I was pleased with the result but Joss was right, I needed to have something about Mrs Forrest herself, the last Darkwater resident. I wondered if I should follow Joss's advice and ring Margaret Hill, choosing the same time as yesterday when Mrs Forrest had been resting. That would be sneaky, but perhaps I'd do better with her amiable, gushing friend.

While I pondered the morals of this idea, I rang the number Bob had written with the name John Curtis.

'Save the Paddington water tower,' the voice at the other end announced crisply.

'Eh?' I was startled. 'Why?'

'Because they're going to pull it down,' my informant told me indignantly, 'and it's a historic landmark. It may not be as old as some and maybe it hasn't been used for years, but it has great historical significance.'

'It has?' I pursued.

'Absolutely. It was built in 1926, you know, to serve the higher areas around Paddington, and now the council wants to demolish it. Why? You may well ask.' I hadn't but he took it as read. 'There's nothing wrong with it, no structural damage, no engineering faults. Just because it's not needed for water any more, knock it down. Typical bureaucratic thinking! Can you imagine the skyline without the old tower? This is the headquarters for the campaign to save it,' he added belatedly.

'Er—great, but I wanted a John Curtis,' I floundered.

'At your service,' he said cheerfully. 'Now, we have a petition which all concerned residents are being urged to sign. Which area are you in? I'll give you the nearest location to register your protest.'

'Well, er, it's great that you're doing something to save the poor old tower, but that's not what I rang about.'

'Oh, I see. Sorry. We rather assume at the moment, you know. How can I help you?'

'Actually, I'm not sure.' I felt I wasn't doing this at all well, and pulled myself together. 'Your name and phone number were written on a friend's—er—blotter, and—look, do you know Bob Slater? Of the *Paddington News*?'

'Of course I know Bob. We go back quite a way. He's doing a piece on the tower for us, to publicize our campaign.'

'Oh. Nothing else?'

'Not that I know of.' Curtis was sounding a little terse. 'Look, would you mind telling me what this is about? I'm a little snowed under at the moment.'

'Bob Slater died yesterday morning,' I said briefly. 'I assume you didn't know, so I'm sorry to have to, well, drop it on you like this.'

'My God! Bob's dead? How? Tuesday, you said?'

I told him. It took him a while to take it in.

'Well, well, poor old Bob! You know, he rang me on Monday afternoon. Asked if he could see me on Tuesday. Said he might have something interesting for me. When he didn't turn up I assumed whatever it was had fallen through and, being tied up with the tower campaign, I didn't think any more about it. I'm sorry, I don't know your name, Mr—?'

'Douglas,' I supplied. 'Michael Douglas.'

'Not *the* Michael Douglas? Our resident famous author?' He sounded delighted. 'Well, well, you do the district proud, Mr Douglas.'

'It's Micky,' I told him. 'You seem to know me but we haven't met, have we?'

He chuckled. 'Oh, I know all about anything of importance in the western suburbs,' he said complacently. 'I'm a historian. I've been writing the history of the area for many years. I keep my eye on the comings and goings around the place. I'm at Ashgrove now, but I used to live in Paddington. That's where I first developed my interest. What my wife Muriel calls my mania.'

This sounded excellent. 'Do you know about a place at Bardon called Darkwater?' I asked urgently.

'Oh yes, the infamous Darkwater. Fascinating place, bloody history. Bob was doing a story on it, I believe.'

I explained my involvement.

'And now I need more information about the present Mrs Forrest, but I don't like to ask her,' I finished awkwardly. 'This pressing people for their private details isn't much in my line.'

'My dear boy, come and see me. I know all about the Fanatical Forrest,' he enthused—a slight case of a pot calling a kettle black! 'I'll tell you everything you want to know about the family.'

I was relieved not to have to disturb the ladies of Darkwater and entered quite cheerfully into another round of 'front door, back door' with Carnie before I went to visit John Curtis.

CHAPTER 8

I drove through the damp, tree-lined streets of Ashgrove, slowing down in Curtis's street to watch for his house. I needn't have bothered. A large sign on his gate proclaimed 'Save The Paddington Water Tower Headquarters'.

His front garden was a riot of wet colour with golden cassias, a bush of bright purple lassiandra and several of what I call Bird of Paradise bushes, covered with red and yellow flowers with their long feathery stamens. Everything was dripping and the cassias dropped damp blossoms with every gust of wind. A pink coralita vine blossomed over a side fence, twining around the palings and casting a hungry eye into the neighbour's yard, probably figuring out how to sneak across without being cut back. Several noisy miners, big birds with nasty yellow eyes and long, sharp beaks, were stripping the dark red berries from a tall umbrella tree, taking advantage of a sudden lull in the attack from the wet skies.

The Curtis house was an old Queenslander set on high stumps, the underneath built in for extra living or storage space. The front steps were one of those impressive affairs comprising a single flight which branched half way down into two opposite sets, giving you a choice of which side you wanted to come up. The path divided around a pretty golden ash tree which was beginning to mess up the closely mown grass with dropped, soggy, autumn leaves.

John Curtis was a vigorous man in his sixties, tall and wiry, with the tanned leather skin of an outdoor lover. He shook my hand warmly and shepherded me into the front room which had once been a wide verandah but was now enclosed. This was obviously the workroom for the tower campaigners as several folding card tables had been pushed together to make one long work bench and were stacked with leaflets, posters and petition forms.

'Through here.' John led the way along the central passageway to an internal staircase. 'My study is downstairs. Used to be a rumpus room when the kids were at home but now we use it for entertaining, and I've claimed a space for all my material. What my wife Muriel calls my junk.'

The downstairs area was concreted over and covered with carpet tiles. A bar and small fridge indicated the social section and several old, comfortable armchairs and a couple of vinyl bean bags were scattered about. A door gave on to a wide back yard with fruit trees, pawpaws, bananas and mandarins, and a barbecue against the back fence.

Part of the room had been partitioned off and John opened the door to this area and pointed me through into his study. The walls were covered in bookshelves crowded with books and manuscripts. He gestured me to a white cane chair and pulled another across for himself.

'Can I get you a beer, Micky? It's a muggy day.'

I accepted and sipped the ice-cold liquid while John talked.

'Eileen Forrest? There's a toughie for you. She's the only survivor of Michael's kids. She had an elder brother, James, who was killed in World War Two and there was another boy, William, five years younger than her, who was drowned in a fishing accident. Michael was Andrew's boy and you know Andrew was the son of the original William?'

I nodded. My ears had pricked up at this evidence of a third William Forrest. I'd taken out my notebook and was trying to keep up with John.

'Right. Starting from scratch, you've got William Forrest, his son Andrew, his son Michael, his daughter Eileen. That's her line to the founder. You want a run-down on her from the beginning?'

'Please. The high spots, anyway.'

'Not a problem. She was born Eileen Amelia Forrest at

Darkwater in 1915. Her father was a magistrate, pretty well
known although I don't expect *you've* heard of him. Well
before your time. He was a bit of a ladies' man, very
handsome fellow. Her mother you will have heard of, rather
a famous lady, one Dorothy May. Right to the fore on
women's reforms—of course she had her husband's Aunt
Charlotte encouraging her like mad. Dorothy May wrote
rather good poetry and had a couple of novels published,
too. She was *always* called Dorothy May. No one ever dared
to shorten her name to a more bite-sized mouthful.'

'I've heard of her,' I said, and then remembered. 'My
great-aunt has her poetry. I've read some of it.'

'Yes, it's good, readable stuff, mostly women's lib, except
they didn't call it that in those days. Poor Michael was
caught between two tough gals.' John chuckled. 'Dorothy
May was a strong, domineering woman, Charlotte likewise.
Charlotte never married, just lived at Darkwater, making
life hell for her magistrate nephew on women's issues. No
wonder the poor bloke was a bit of a weakling and easily
led, so they say, and took his pleasures elsewhere; but he
had his share of family pride, like they all did.'

'I had the impression Mrs Forrest was a bit, well, fanatical,' I put in. 'Not so much that she keeps the house as a
period piece—after all, there's nothing wrong with preserv-
ing history—but I thought she carried family pride a little
too far, and the way she talked I kept expecting her ancestors
to knock at the door and come home.'

'Oh, she's as mad as a hatter, but quite harmless,' John
said cheerfully, 'about the family, anyway. Can't blame her,
she was fed Forrest Family Tradition for breakfast, dinner
and tea. Always taught to put loyalty and duty to the family
first. You know their motto?'

'I saw it over the gate. In Latin.'

'Roughly translated it says, "Together united in victory".
A bit scary when you think what a bit of fanaticism could
do with that.'

'I'd be a hopeless reporter,' I lamented. 'There was so much I didn't think to ask. I just let her talk and took what she told me.'

'She's a bit overpowering,' John agreed, 'but it's not a problem. We'll see what we can do. None of this is secret, by the way, you could get it easily from a number of sources. Now, school. She went to Somerville House, nothing but the best for the Forrests. Their fortune is immense. She went on to Uni where she studied medicine. She also had a keen interest in botany. Must have caught it from the first William. He was an enthusiastic amateur and messed about with experiments, trying to find cures for diseases and things—without much success, I believe.'

'Tell me about Mrs Forrest's husband,' I said. 'Margaret Hill mentioned his death but wouldn't say anything about it.'

'Mmmm, probably terrified Eileen would overhear.' John grinned. 'Cliff was actually a mate of mine and his death was a bit of a shock to us all. He shot himself after his son's funeral. He'd gone totally to pieces, poor devil. Thought he'd been responsible for Bill's death.'

I paused in my rapid scribbling. 'Good God, what happened?'

'Well, Bill was twenty-five, studying law, following in Cliff's footsteps. Cliff was a barrister. A bloody good one. He knew a devious trick or two. You know what his colleagues used to call him? The Mountie, because he always got his man.' He laughed at the memory. 'Bill wasn't living at Darkwater but he visited all the time. He and Cliff were at loggerheads about something. Don't know what, a family matter, probably. Anyway, one night young Bill went up to the house, had an unholy row with Cliff and slammed out. He had an MG sports car. It was a wet night and he skidded off the road and crashed at the bottom of Kaye Street. Like poor old Bob Slater. Cliff took on a load of guilt and blamed himself. He loved Bill. They had another two kids but Bill was his father's favourite. After the funeral he went to his room. Everyone thought he'd gone to lie down. Then we heard a pistol shot and found he'd committed suicide. Eileen was hit hard, in her own way. Took it with icy calm but she dropped the Trent part of her name and never spoke of him again, as far as I know. It was a bad business.'

'A shame,' I agreed. 'That explains Margaret's caution.'

It also gave me another William, Bill Trent, late son of Eileen. Well, I knew how he died, and Eileen's brother William; both accidental deaths.

'There are a lot of Williams in the Forrest saga,' I commented hopefully.

'Well, of course. Named for the first William. It's a popular Forrest name.'

'What happened to the first William?' I asked casually. 'And his son, William Junior, Margaret Jane's son?'

'Funnily enough, it's a very similar story,' John said slowly. 'Now I come to think of it, it's damned strange. William Junior inherited his father's love of adventure and couldn't settle down at Darkwater and follow in his father's footsteps, which was a bit of a blow to Will Senior, as you can imagine. When Will Junior was in his early thirties gold was discovered in Western Australia, the Kimberleys, and William just had to be there. To seek his fortune, although his father's own fortune could have kept him in silk shirts for the rest of his life. But he was William's son and wanted to do his own thing, so off he went. He did make a fortune, too, and came back five years later, only to be killed almost immediately.'

'How was he killed?' Was this the death that had interested Bob?

'A tree fell on him,' John said briefly. 'He was clearing some bush on the Darkwater perimeter—this would have been in 1891. A tree just fell the wrong way and he was too slow to move. His father was devastated. He began to suffer bouts of ill health and his temper, always on a short fuse, got worse and worse. He also suffered fits of depression. One day he took a gun and went out, to shoot crows, he said. They found him by the well, a bullet in his brain. Of course it was hushed up, just another accident in a long line for the unlucky family. But it's accepted now that he killed himself.'

'But he was such a strong man,' I said, and added hastily, 'from what I hear!'

'Yes, he was. He'd been through the worst life could throw at him in the way of personal tragedy and he'd never quit. But there were rumours that his mind had begun to go and one of the family friends wrote a letter which I managed to see and photocopy many years ago, saying that just before he ended his life he'd been seen by the well, presumably talking to himself and in great distress, beating at the air with his fists and clutching his head. It was a servant who'd seen him and she said he was raving. She thought he was talking to someone and went out to see, but there wasn't anyone else there. So she turned to go back into the house and she heard the shot.'

There was a long silence.

'And Amelia?' I asked at last.

'Oh, she lived on for many years at Darkwater, kept to herself a lot, but died of old age and peacefully. One of the few Forrests to do so.'

He looked across at me and his face was sad.

'It's a tragic family,' he said, almost to himself. 'People say they're unlucky. I've always thought they must be cursed, or something.'

CHAPTER 9

Muriel Curtis was a brisk woman in her early sixties with bright eyes and grey hair set in crisp waves. She wore an old suede skirt and no-nonsense walking shoes. She appeared at the study door, explained she'd been out letterbox-dropping water tower leaflets, and took tea and coffee orders.

'Tell me about Adrian Forrest,' I asked John as Muriel left us with drinks and a plate of sandwiches. She'd reminded us it was past lunch-time and invited me to a scratch meal. The sandwiches were delicious. Muriel was an efficient lady.

He grinned at me. 'What did *she* tell you about him?'

'Mrs Forrest? Nothing, really. She showed me miniatures of the children and intimated that Adrian was a bit of a dead loss. She said he never really belonged. I thought he had a nice face.'

'That's probably why he didn't fit,' John said. 'He hadn't the Forrest features or temperament and dropped the family completely when he left. As far as I know the two branches still don't visit or communicate.'

'Why? What was the trouble?'

'It's a bit of a nasty story. Have another sandwich. I think these are curried something—egg, maybe. The first William was a typical white man of the times, with a typical invader's mentality. The blacks, you see. Had no time for them. The English mind couldn't comprehend. The natives didn't cultivate the land and grow crops—they must be completely useless and primitive. Never mind that the aborigines had a rare and extensive understanding of the bush and wildlife and lived almost in luxury with a range of foods that would shame the European diet. The whites hadn't the nous to learn from the blacks, just tried to superimpose England on to the Australian bush. They didn't even realize the blacks had a complete language. Assumed they were intellectually retarded because they thought the language was very meagre and only went as far as simple basic needs and wants. It was much later they realized it was as complex as any other. When it was too late, of course.'

'Margaret mentioned trouble with the blacks on ball nights,' I put in.

'Yes, Darkwater had more than the normal strife and that was down to William Senior. He despised the blacks, wanted nothing to do with them, thought of them as no better than wild animals and vermin at that. There was a camp of blacks nearby when he bought the land, but they disappeared. That's how Darkwater got its name, you know. There was a waterhole which was used by the blacks. Used to be known as the blacks' water, then Blackwater, later Darkwater. I expect William ran them off.'

'Would he have mentioned it in his diary?' I asked. 'Mrs Forrest talked about him keeping one.'

'Yes, but the earliest diary's missing,' John said sadly. 'I've seen the others, but they date from after he built Darkwater.'

I wondered how a family as concerned about its history as the Forrests could have lost the founder's diary. Meanwhile, John was filling me in on the problems with the natives. He told me Brisbane was generally noted for its lack of trouble. There were very few tribes, which was one of the reasons the site was chosen in the first place and the blacks rarely came near the white settlement. What encounters there were were generally friendly. Most trouble came from convicts ill-treating the natives, and settlers like William.

'What did he do?'

'Well, he planted vegetable gardens, of course, not having a clue how to live off the land. All the settlers did the same and the natives began to lose interest in their own bush tucker and want this exotic European stuff. So they took to raiding the gardens.' He sighed. 'The whites hadn't bothered to understand how the blacks lived. The aboriginal was a communal dweller, he had no concept of personal ownership. Everything was shared by the tribe. Food was shared, kids looked after by everyone so they had a big extended family and there was always someone there for them. No neglected children. William thought they were stealing, of course, not realizing the blacks had no idea what that was but were simply taking what they saw as communal food. He set patrols in the gardens and in one raid they fired on and killed several natives.'

I shook my head in sympathy. 'A sad business.'

'Typical. William had no compunction about firing on any aboriginals around Darkwater.'

'Mrs Forrest said they'd mostly died out by 1860.'

'True. The whites brought them civilization, VD, prostitution, diseases like smallpox and measles to which they had no resistance. They hadn't a chance, poor bastards. There were about three hundred blacks of the same tribe on the north side of the river, living in more or less separate family groups with their own territories. They were virtually extinct by the 'sixties. Well, they're gone now. The aboriginals in Brisbane today aren't locals. We've lost most of their lore, their culture—no one thought it was worth while to record it—well, very few enlightened souls. It's a shame, Micky, and we're the losers. If you aren't going to have those corned beef ones, I'll have them.'

I pushed the plate over and he ate in silence then drained his cup and went to the door.

'Muriel,' he called, 'Muriel, love, how about another cuppa?'

'You're not still boring Micky to death with your old yarns?' she called back. 'Tell him I'll keep an eye out and rescue him if you stay down there too long.'

John came back, chuckling. 'Now, where were we? Oh yes, Adrian. That was how I got on to the aboriginals.

Adrian, I'm afraid, was the bane of William's life over the blacks. He was one of the rare ones. Made friends with them, learned the Turribal language, traded blankets and meat for wild honey and fish and twine. He even started a collection of artifacts—spears, boomerangs, stone knives, hatchets, that sort of thing. Then he committed the greatest sin of all. There was one family he got close to and he and an aboriginal boy of his own age used to go swimming together. Once the boy got into difficulties and would have drowned, but Adrian saved him. Well, he had an affair with the boy's sister. William did his block. Disowned him completely. They'd always clashed over William's attitude to the blacks. There'd been another time some years earlier when Adrian left, but he came back later.'

'What happened?' I asked.

'Darkwater was always plagued by marauding natives. Not just raiding the gardens but attacking the house. They seemed to have a special hatred for it. One night there was an unsuccessful attack and William shot two men and captured three others. He locked them in the coach house. Then, being a JP, he held a trial in his own house the next day, passed sentence on them and hanged them from a tree on his own property.'

'Could he do that?' I was startled.

'He bloody did it! Who was going to stop him?'

'So Adrian left home.'

'But came back, as I said. Loyalty to the family, love of Amelia, who knows? But it got too much for him in the end and he never came back to Darkwater; and, may I say, his side of the family has flourished like a blooming great eucalypt by a billabong. It drove William crazy to see Adrian so successful and happy away from Darkwater.'

'It seems that only the Forrests who stayed at Darkwater were unlucky, then,' I commented.

He grinned. 'Looks that way. Maybe the curse is on the place, not the people.'

I was curious. 'Who told you all this?'

He gave me a mysterious look and said, 'Adrian'.

I nodded. 'Oh sure, just like that. Adrian Forrest told you all about himself.'

'In a way, yes.' He was enjoying my puzzlement. 'But not face to face; through his diaries.'

'Aha! Thank God for that!'

He laughed. 'When I got interested in the Forrest story, I wondered about Adrian, same as you did. Eileen wasn't forthcoming so I contacted Belgara, Adrian's station and the present owner, Christopher Forrest, let me read the diaries. Adrian wrote the whole story.'

Muriel joined us with more hot drinks.

'It's teeming again,' she said cheerfully. 'Thank God for the clothes drier. Normally I'd say it's good for the garden, but the ground's so waterlogged the water's just running off.'

'I was pleased to see your ash tree,' I told her. 'Suitable for the suburb.'

'Ashgrove? Of course there never was an ash grove. So many of our places were named by homesick settlers after their familiar English districts, as I'm sure John will tell you.'

'Ashgrove, Red Hill, Bardon,' John nodded. 'Named from Bardon House, which of course Jeays named for Bardon Hill in Leicestershire.'

I nodded. Bardon House is one of our historical houses, now part of a Catholic school. It's registered with the National Trust and has their blue plaque of approval affixed to it. It was built by Joshua Jeays, architect, builder, quarry master and later Mayor of Brisbane. Sadly, though, Jeays never lived in the house that he built. His beloved wife died before it was completed and he gave it to his son. Couldn't face living there alone.

John shrugged. 'No imagination, the pioneers,' he complained. 'I like the aboriginal names best. They've got some meaning to them. Mount Coot-tha, for instance, from *ku-ta*, the wild native honey.' He got up and went to rummage through his desk drawers.

'I've got some photographs of Cliff and Eileen. Yes, here they are. Just family snapshots. Here's Eileen on the lawn at Darkwater with Bill. He's about two or three there. The other woman is Margaret. Margaret Blake she was then. She married late, and her husband only lived a few more years. Died of influenza. He was Jerry Hill. She was always at Darkwater. Adored Eileen.' He shuffled the photos. 'This is Cliff, in his barrister's get-up. Looks very legal. Here, you can look through them.'

I took the bundle and began to examine the snaps, when I remembered the other thing I'd come about.

'Does the name "Deathwater" mean anything to you?'

John looked at me with a slightly startled expression. 'Now, where did you hear that one? Not from Eileen, I know.'

'No, Bob Slater had jotted it down on his blotter. We thought it must be something to do with Darkwater.'

He cocked an intelligent eye at me. '"We" who? Joss Bates? Well, you were right. It's the name that's been around for many years. One doesn't say it to the Forrests. Probably came about because of all the deaths. I didn't realize it was still known or used.'

I'd gone back to the photographs. One attracted me—a young man with a 'fifties short back and sides, a cheerful face with The Nose, and a pipe in his mouth.

'Who's this?' I held it up for John's inspection.

'Ah, that's Bill Trent, Cliff and Eileen's son. That must have been taken about five years before he was killed.' He looked fondly at the face in the snapshot. 'He was a cheeky young devil. See that pipe of his? Eileen hated it. She disapproved of smoking and wouldn't let Bill light up in the house. Said the smell of it turned her stomach.' He laughed suddenly at the memory. 'Bill was as stubborn as she was and when they argued it was the clash of the Titans all right! He used to get his own way by sneaking down to the servants' quarters, which were used as store rooms, and smoke down there. He reckoned that was still in the house. I expect Eileen knew, though. You couldn't keep anything from her.' He stopped and looked keenly at me. 'What's wrong, Micky?'

I'm not ashamed to admit that a cold shiver was using my spine as a xylophone.

'Eileen showed me around the servants' quarters,' I said reluctantly. 'There was a scent in the air which was faint, but recognizable. It was pipe smoke.'

Muriel gave a startled exclamation but John just sat there, not moving, a grave expression on his face.

'Was there so?' he said oddly. 'That's very interesting. That's very interesting indeed.'

CHAPTER 10

I sat cross-legged on Al Wang's carpet and sipped a cup of steaming fragrant Chinese tea. Opposite, Al's gentle moon face beamed at me. The flat, with its bright cushions, carved oriental screen, a scattering of little jade ornaments and the faint scent of incense, always has a calm atmosphere which never fails to soothe me. It emanates from Al, who carries an aura of serenity about with him. He explained to me once that this was because he always knew where his spine was. All I know is that he's easy to be with.

He watched me now with interest and shook his head slowly back and forth.

'What has happened to disturb you, my friend?'

I set down my cup, unsure of how to proceed. Finally I said bluntly, 'Al, do you believe in ghosts?'

He gave me an open, guileless look. 'I am Chinese,' he said simply. 'Naturally I believe in ghosts. It's our tradition.' Then, in all seriousness, 'Are you having trouble with a restless spirit?'

I never know when he's putting me on. His innocent look's his most dangerous. He has a quiet, mad sense of humour with which he leads people up interminable garden paths. You have to watch him.

'You mean you honestly believe that a place can be haunted?'

He smiled gently. 'Naturally, as a man of the twentieth century, living in a scientific age, I do not believe such things. I am aware that all ghostly phenomena may be explained by reason. However, as a Chinese with many generations of understanding at my disposal of matters which you Westerners have never properly grasped, I tell you again, Michael, yes, I believe in ghosts and that a place may be haunted.' He paused and looked at me carefully. 'You'd better tell me. I may be able to help.'

'I doubt it. I think I'm probably going off my rocker, but how else do I explain the odd feeling of—no, evil is probably too strong—I'll say disquiet; and that damned pipe smoke?'

'Tell me,' Al invited again. 'This sounds most interesting.'

I told him about Darkwater, my odd, shivery feelings, the sense of relief when I left, the smell of smoke in the servants' quarters and how Bill had died.

'It's an eerie coincidence,' I said, and shook myself as an odd feeling of doom gripped me, 'for Bill Trent and Bob Slater to come to grief in the same place.' A rain-laden wind gust rattled the windows and I started slightly, then felt like a fool.

'Michael, I have told you before, there is no such thing as coincidence,' Al sighed. 'The Universe is not so randomly run. All events move in an orderly fashion, each linked to the other. There is meaning in all of life, if you will only pause to look. If you had said it was synchronistic, it would have been more accurate.'

I shrugged. Coincidence, synchronicity, it was still a hell of a long shot that two people coming from Darkwater on a wet night both bought it by the Governor's back fence.

'If this Bill Trent died with matters still to be dealt with, troubles still unsolved, perhaps because of the fight with his father, his presence may very well be felt at Darkwater still. Unresolved matters can cause a spirit confusion and bind it to the Earth plane.' Al sounded as if this was merely another of life's routine events.

'You mean, he could still be wandering round the servants' quarters *smoking a pipe* because he's upset about his dad?' It was all too much for my scientific Western mind. 'How does he stop the pipe from falling through him? That was real smoke, Al.'

He turned on his Oriental inscrutability look. 'It is a well known phenomenon, familiar scents happening with visitations,' he said. 'A woman's perfume, the scent of flowers, even pipe smoke. Michael, let go your logic and reason and listen to your feelings. You have good instincts, trust them. Your feelings told you something was amiss at this place. You knew instinctively that there was an atmosphere of disquiet.'

I was silent. I couldn't argue that one.

'Any atmosphere may be imprinted by emotions, deeply held feelings, loves and hatreds,' Al went on earnestly. 'The very stuff of the walls absorbs such impressions. You must have entered rooms that "felt" peaceful to you, or others that you felt uncomfortable to be in. Perhaps you have said, "This is an unhappy place," or "This is a place of great grief." We all experience these feelings, often in the most unexpected places; then we say, "What nonsense, this is irrational," and in so doing, we deny the reality of our subtle senses which are far more attuned to the atmosphere around us than we would like to admit.'

He was right. Witness the serenity of his room. I didn't imagine that. Everyone at No. 18 had commented on it at some time or another.

'Think about it.' Al smiled. 'There are ways of contacting and releasing such unhappy spirits. I know a woman who could help.'

'OK, Al, thanks.' One of us was crazy. I hated to think it might be me.

Back in my flat I dialled the police headquarters again and made tentative inquiries about Bob. Could they tell me if he'd been drinking? What information could they give me about his accident?

'Are you a relative?' the constable asked. She sounded nice. Husky voice.

Unfortunately I cut no ice with her and after a lengthy argument she more or less told me to get lost.

Nothing daunted, I tried another number. The phone was answered on the first ring.

'Inspector Reeves's desk,' the voice said briskly.

'Is the Inspector available?'

'Yeah, hang on.' Then: 'David, your phone, mate.'

'Coming!' I waited, listening through the receiver to the rain drumming on the police roof, like an ever-present background rumble. Through it came a familiar, calm voice.

'David Reeves.'

'Michael Douglas,' I countered.

'Micky! Well, well. Solved any more murders lately?'

'Ha-ha!' I said politely. 'Who's a funny detective, then?'

I could hear the twinkle in his voice. 'What can I do for you?'

I told him about Bob. 'They won't give me any info, David, and all I really want to know is if Bob was back on the grog. I went down Kaye Street. The silly bastard was coming down the wrong side of the road by the skid mark. I thought, if it's not a state secret, you could find out for me—if it's OK to ask you, of course.'

'I remember Bob Slater from his crime reporting days,' David Reeves said thoughtfully. 'Good bloke, complete professional, great integrity. I'll get back to you, Micky.'

I've always said it pays to have a friend in the force. An hour later he rang back.

'Autopsy results negative on the alcohol,' he told me. 'Bob was as sober as a judge.'

I was relieved, but puzzled. 'Did they say anything about the car? It wasn't brakes or steering, or anything?'

'What's the matter, Micky? Have you let that curiosity of yours out of the bag? Accident people say no, the car was sound, tyre tread legal and safe.'

I didn't want to ask, but I needed to know. 'David, he couldn't have been on drugs, could he?'

'He was tested. They automatically look for anything like that—and of course they picked up the skid marks, so they were well alert. He was clean.'

'Then you tell me,' I said, almost angrily, 'how a sober

man, in a mechanically sound vehicle, could have been driving down the wrong side of the road and skidded into the fence like that?'

He paused and the rain crackled in the line connecting us. Then his voice was gentle. 'Micky, let it go,' he advised. 'Look, it was a wet night, there was a spate of accidents on Monday. Visibility was lousy. It's a steep incline and we know from Miss Bates that Bob Slater drove too fast. If he was tired, just a moment's inattention; and, in that area, a possum could've run across the road, or a cat or dog—he could have swerved to avoid it. It's accidental death, Micky.'

'Yes, I expect you're right,' I agreed reluctantly. 'I had a bad feeling about it, David, but you're right. It must have been an accident; just rotten luck.'

I heard a soft squeaking. David was swinging his swivel chair from side to side, a familiar habit when he was thinking something through. 'There was something,' he said at last. 'A couple of the people from the houses opposite, who raised the alarm, said a car drove off. It had been parked a little way up the hill and took off as they got to the wreck. In the dark and the rain no one could give a description, no one saw the driver. It's believed that a passing motorist saw the car, stopped with the idea of helping, then, seeing the people coming out of the houses, left the scene, not wanting to be involved. The radio and papers have appealed on our behalf for anyone with information to come forward. Bob might have swerved to avoid that vehicle.'

'Then he'd still have to have been on the wrong side of the road,' I pointed out.

'Yes. The theory that he was trying to avoid an animal still holds.'

I couldn't think of a reasonable alternative.

'When's Bob's funeral?' David asked, breaking the silence.

'Tomorrow, ten a.m. Toowong Cemetery.'

'I'll try to get there. Be nice if some of the blokes who

knew him from the old days could show up. I'll mention it around.'

I checked my watch as Reeves rang off. Joss wouldn't be back for ages. I left a note on the door, dropped the key in with Monica Wainwright, owner, caretaker and den mother of the flats, and went to see my favourite relative.

Melanie Carter-Jones is my great-aunt, but don't spread it around. She says it makes her feel old, and she's anything but that. Age has nothing to do with it, so she tells me. You're only as old as you feel. These days all she'll admit is that she's over seventy. She's tall for her generation, five foot nine, and beautiful with it. Carries herself like a duchess. Silver hair, fine-boned face, eyes between blue and violet and sharp as they ever were. She misses nothing. An amazing lady in many ways.

You might say Laney educated me. She's the best relative I have, and I followed her around like a puppy when I was a kid. She fostered my imagination, taught me to look at the world with something akin to her own childlike wonder and took me in as a boarder when I disgraced myself by turning my back on my father's world of cash books, journals and desk chains and decided to write for a living. 'Throwing your education away,' he moaned in disbelief. He's still not convinced that what I do is productive work and expects some sort of retribution to catch up with me any day now. Needless to say, Laney supported me enthusiastically.

'You can stop looking daggers at me, Stephen,' she advised my father at my twenty-first, after my surprise announcement. He'd accurately sheeted the blame home to Laney. 'He's a big boy now and he can do what he damn well likes!' She filled her champagne glass and toasted me flamboyantly, while the family struggled with the words that seemed to have stuck invisibly in their throats. If we'd had a fireplace, I swear she'd have smashed the glass triumphantly into it.

Laney lives in an old colonial, circa 1860, on a hilltop

overlooking the busy Brisbane River. The road is wide and tree-lined and a stand of huge weeping figs at the bottom of the hill makes a good shelter from sun or rain where you park your car to save it the trouble of struggling up the impossibly steep driveway to her house. You walk up. Laney's visitors have to be of athletic bent to make it to the front door.

The river was grey and pounded flat by the wall of water falling on it. In the late afternoon the rain made everything misty. There were no low-flying planes swooping in across the cargo ships moored at the nearby wharves. The airport was closed, due to flooding.

Laney's house was a typical colonial model. The earliest Australian buildings, designed and constructed by English architects and builders, were copies of the Georgian designs they'd been used to back in the old country, in spite of their being totally unsuited to Aussie conditions. Eventually, however, they woke up to themselves and a new style evolved, built for maximum coolth. It became the norm for inner rooms to have access to wide verandahs, and houses began to sprawl across their grounds in a way unheard of in crowded English cities, as the pioneers took advantage of more space than they knew what to do with.

Laney's house wasn't as old as Darkwater but it certainly had a more cheerful atmosphere, and a porch where Laney had thoughtfully left a towel for me. I dried off and rang her bell.

CHAPTER 11

John Curtis had told me as much as I needed about Eileen Forrest to complete my story, but from what he'd said, I knew someone who could give me even more personal details. And I wanted to know about the Forrests and their home, and Bob's cryptic doodle.

Laney and I watched the grey rain curtain over the river from the sanctuary of her lounge room.

'You went to Somerville House,' I said. 'Do you remember an Eileen Forrest? She's about your age, so she might have been in your class.'

'Aha! I knew this was more than a casual visit.' Laney's all-seeing eyes twinkled. 'But why on earth do you want to know about Eileen?'

I gave her a brief outline.

'Then Curtis mentioned your old school and I thought . . .'

'You thought I could spill even more intimate beans than he could? Well, you're right. Mind you, I haven't seen Eileen for many years, so I don't know what she's up to these days. I remember Darkwater well as a girl. Wonderful balls and parties, and us young things all vying for the attention of Eileen's brothers. Both tall, good-looking Forrest men. Goodness, that takes me back! James and William.'

'Do you remember how William died?'

'Oh yes, it was a terrible accident. I was supposed to have been there myself, but my mother wasn't well that weekend, so I stayed at home.'

'Tell me about it, Laney. It was just an accident, wasn't it?'

'Yes, Micky, there were many witnesses; not what you're

looking for, dear. A party of young people went away for the weekend. Now, now, Micky. We were *very* well chaperoned in those days. The Forrests had a weekender at the coast. On the Sunday morning, several of the party went fishing from the rocks. Very dangerous; there was a big surf, but those Forrest boys were always daredevils and egging each other on. Macho, they'd say, these days. William was swept off the rocks by a wave and they didn't find his body until it was washed ashore two days later. There was never any doubt that it was an accident, so if it was that William, your friend was on the wrong track.'

'I see. Well, I've still got three other Darkwater Williams.'

Laney was watching me closely. 'Is it just for Joss that you're doing this?'

I shook my head. No use lying to Laney—she knows me too well.

'No, love, you've sprung me again. I'm rather interested myself. Look, I've been doing some serious thinking. Bob's death was strange. Yes, I know he drove like a bat out of hell, but he knew when to let it rip and when to be careful. I don't believe he'd have been speeding down Kaye—and on the wrong side of the road, yet!—on a dark, wet night; but there it is. He wasn't drunk, the car was sound. David Reeves thinks he swerved to avoid an animal.'

'It's very likely, dear,' Laney said gently. 'Why does it worry you so much?'

'Because—' I hesitated, not sure I wasn't making a bloody great clown of myself—'because, very recently, while he was researching a story about Darkwater, he wrote on a brand-new blotter, "How did William really die?" and worked around it with arrows while he was having a good think about things. Then on Monday he told John Curtis, a local historian, he might have something interesting for him the next day, and on Monday night he crashed before he could say what it was, just coincidentally, coming back from dinner at Darkwater.'

'Micky!' She was startled. 'What on earth are you suggesting?'

'Nothing,' I sighed, 'because it isn't possible, because Bob *would* have swerved to miss a possum on the road and what he wanted to tell Curtis may have had nothing whatever to do with Darkwater. Come to think of it, he was doing a piece for John on the history of the Paddington water tower, so it was probably about that. Forget it, Laney. I'm out of my tree.'

There was a hint of sternness in the look she gave me. 'It sounds to me as if your imagination is getting away from you. You came close to making a very serious accusation.'

I held out my hand. 'I know, love, I'm sorry. And Eileen Forrest is a friend of yours.'

She patted my hand and smiled a little. 'She wasn't one of my closest friends, but I—er—did her a favour once. She had a great deal of family pride and I, well, kept a secret that would have disgraced her family if it had become known. She always said she was in my debt.'

'What on earth was it?'

Laney pursed her lips. 'I can't tell you that. It wouldn't be fair to Eileen.'

I know better than to beat my head against a brick wall. 'All right, but tell me about her as you remember.'

'Well, as you know, we were at school together and I visited Darkwater a lot in those days. They had a marvellous ballroom with a properly sprung floor, so the dances were very popular, and the brothers, as I said. I was very keen on James at one time, so I made sure I was nice to Eileen so I'd keep getting invited.'

'Tut, tut!' I admonished her.

'Yes, I know, it wasn't very kind of me to use her like that, but we all did it. Eileen was very popular.'

'Laney, I'm shocked!'

She laughed. 'I gave up on James when I realized he preferred to play the field, and then I met your Uncle Robert and fell in love with him. We'd been married for a year when Eileen married Clifford Trent. They'd met at University. Clifford was a law student. A very staid sort of boy, took himself far too seriously. They were married in 1938 and, when the war broke out the next year, Clifford joined the Air Force and Eileen and I and many of our friends decided to work for the war effort. Of course, with the Americans stationed here, there was a lot to do. Darkwater was occupied in 1942 as a convalescent home for the American soldiers. It was a very different sort of place then. The ballroom was turned into a hospital ward and all the paintings and ornaments were packed up.' She sighed. 'James went off to war and was killed. Everything was going to belong to Eileen, when her parents died.'

'I imagine Darkwater couldn't have had a better mistress.'

'No, indeed. After the war she threw herself into restoring the house to the way it had been. Clifford came home and took up law again, and became a barrister. Before he died, you know, he'd been in line for a knighthood. Eileen must have been very proud, but now, with all the scandal coming out at the Fitzgerald Inquiry, it makes me wonder. So many Government supporters seem to have been given these honours as rewards for nothing more than large contributions to the Party and suchlike.'

I nodded. After years of Government corruption, and ditto the police and the legal profession, the Government had finally been forced to open an Inquiry, headed by Tony Fitzgerald, QC. It had been under way for ten months and had already brought down the Premier and some of his senior ministers. We'd have been shocked by all the allegations if it hadn't been common knowledge for more years than we could remember.

'Eileen was wonderful for Clifford,' Laney went on. 'Unfortunately, he was a bit of a weakling, not unlike Eileen's own father, but she worked as hard for his career as for

Darkwater and he became very successful, if full of his own importance. They had three children, a boy, William John, christened, of course, for the first Forrest, and two girls, Amelia and Charlotte. More family names, you notice.'

'I know William was killed in a car crash,' I put in. 'John Curtis told me the story. He was a friend of the family.'

'I don't remember him,' Laney said, 'but they had many friends. It may have been in later years.'

'What happened to the girls?'

'Amelia married an American. His father had been at Darkwater convalescing and was later killed in the war. His son was doing a sort of pilgrimage around all the places his father had been. He had a snapshot of his father at Darkwater, and letters about the kindness of the family. He looked them up. Amelia lives in California now. The other girl, Charlotte, had a nursery—for plants, dear. She was keen on botany, like her mother. She had a couple of florist shops as well, I believe. She married a man—now, let me think—Dyson? Dyer? No, Dysart, that was it. You'd find her in the phone book, if you wanted any more details.'

'Thanks, love, you've been a terrific help,' I said gratefully.

She looked a little worried. 'Micky, dear, I wish you wouldn't go on with this idea that one of the boys was murdered. It would be very difficult to find out and you could stir up a lot of trouble and hurt people. After all, you said yourself the first William killed himself and his son's death was accidental. I've told you how it was with Eileen's brother, and you know about her son. Your friend Bob probably jumped to an unfounded conclusion. Perhaps he wanted to believe something was wrong, so he could investigate it. Isn't it best to let the past stay in the past?'

'Let sleeping dogs lie, eh?' I grinned at her. 'You're probably right, love. I've got enough on Eileen Forrest to finish Joss's article. I'll get it done and get back to my book. God knows, Alan will have my hide if I don't get on with it.' Alan is my publisher, a nice bloke, but worries about deadlines. 'One thing though, I nearly forgot. Have you ever heard the name "Deathwater"?'

She raised her brows. 'Goodness, I'd forgotten that. Yes, it was something we never said in front of the family, of course, but sometimes someone would refer to Death-water—just joking.'

'Where did the name come from?'

She frowned. 'I don't think I ever knew. It was just another name for the place. A sort of folk name, I suppose. I have an idea it was something to do with the pioneering days, but I don't know what made me think that. How did you hear of it?'

I told her, and John Curtis's explanation. Her brow cleared. 'I expect that's right. Because of all the deaths. I must have been wrong about it going back to the old days.'

When I got home I found Joss breading zucchini strips. She'd made a salad and the table was set. Very homey. Joss is a vegetarian, like me. Everybody's doing it these days, especially now the news is out that the South American rainforests, the lungs of the earth, are being torn down for the hamburger industry. Joss and I were ahead of our time. No one thinks it strange any more, thank God. I used to get tired of explaining that I wasn't a hippie, or gay, or un-Australian.

The rain which had spattered intermittently against the windscreen all the way home in that annoying way it has of not being quite heavy enough to need the wipers but being just too much not to, suddenly made up its mind and drenched me in a thunderous downpour as I raced for the front door.

'You're soaking!' Joss disapproved. People love to state the obvious. 'Oh, Micky, would you close that window? I opened it when the rain wasn't so heavy, to air the flat, but it'll probably be coming in now.' I stood looking out at the grey, soaking world for a moment before I pulled the window shut. It overlooked Princess Road, the huge fig tree with the taste for concrete which grows on the footpath, and the small park opposite. The street lights had come on and were glowing yellow through the murk, lighting the arrows of rain as they slanted by. My attention was caught by something odd. A figure was standing under the lamp-post over the road, and the light picked out the burly figure in a long, dark stockman's coat and wide-brimmed Akubra. All I could see of the face was a long, bushy beard as the man's head was turned up to look at No. 18. I'd have sworn he was scanning the upper floors of the house and drew back instinctively.

'Micky, what on earth are you doing mooning about in those wet clothes?' Joss had joined me with a glass in her hand. 'Have a sherry and go and change, for goodness sake!'

'There's someone over the road, watching the house,' I said briefly, and turned back to the window.'

'I don't see anyone.' Joss peered out.

'Neither do I, now.' The figure had gone. 'But there was a man standing under the lamp-post, looking up here. He must have seen me watching him and took off.'

'Silly!' She closed the window. 'Now the carpet is wet. It was probably just someone walking his dog.'

'In this weather?'

'You've been watching too much television,' she said, laughing at me.

I shrugged. The house is pretty well burglar-proof, but I'd sleep with one eye open. I wonder how you do that? It sounds bloody uncomfortable.

I took Joss's advice and went to dry off. That night I finished the article. Joss was delighted with it and cried a little, thinking of Bob. My duty done, I could write *finis* to the Forrests and their strange, disturbing house. As I was dropping off to sleep, it suddenly occurred to me that John Curtis would know the date of Bill Trent's accident and I could look up the newspaper of the time and see what they said. I honestly wasn't going to get involved and I knew it was an accident, but I'd been thinking. Joss had said Bob spent hours looking up old newspaper reports. Now, if he was sussing out a death, it had to be Bill Trent's. Figure it out. If there'd been newspaper reports of William Junior's death, they'd have had no details, other than what the family wanted the public to know. A powerful man like William Senior wasn't going to splash it about that his son was murdered, if he was. He'd have been more likely to hush it up and take matters into his own hands, finding out the truth and meting out justice himself. Ditto for William Senior. They'd hardly let it be printed that the founder of the Darkwater dynasty went off his rocker and killed himself, if that's what they believed. Any reports would have been of the 'Tragic Accident at Darkwater' variety. Laney had assured me that Eileen's brother's death had been a well-witnessed accident, no suspicious circumstances. The only one of the deaths that would have any sort of story that Bob could have followed up in detail was Bill Trent's accident and inquest. My gut feeling said Bill was the one to watch, the only one that would have made re-investigating worth while. With Bob's contacts it would have been a snip for him to question the police who attended the scene, friends, relatives, etc. I wasn't going as far as that, but it would be interesting just to read about it. My thoughts tailed off and I finally got to sleep, both eyes firmly closed.

CHAPTER 12

Joss left early the next morning to complete Saturday's edition. The *Paddington News* came out twice a week on Wednesdays and Saturdays. I picked her up later and took her to the cemetery.

Bob's funeral was suitably gloomy with a low, heavy sky, and well attended by shocked friends who'd known him from the old days, as well as those from more recent times. Joanna looked elegant and sorrowful in black, and froze Joss with a speaking look before ignoring her completely. Joss had made a hasty round of the local boutiques for some more clothes and wore a grey pleated skirt and silky top. Her face was white with blue shadows under her eyes and she'd obviously not slept much. She held my arm tightly. John Curtis risked Joanna's iré by staying with us; some of the others were unsure of whom to comfort and walked an edgy tightrope between the two women; others were more obvious about where their sympathies lay, openly supporting either Joanna or Joss. It was not a happy occasion. Not that one expects joy at a funeral, but it could have been more comfortable. The sodden grass squelched underfoot and oozed mud which spattered shoes, stockinged ankles and trousers.

David Reeves put in an appearance and had rounded up some of Bob's police friends. They stayed a little aloof from the rest of the crowd, but David's superior height gave him the advantage and he spotted us over the heads between us and eased his lanky frame through the people to say hello. I introduced him to Joss, and he offered his sympathy in the same easy, calm tones I'd heard him using to Joanna a little earlier. A diplomat.

'Glad you could come,' I told him as we gathered at the graveside.

'I was glad to be able to, although this isn't the weather for a graveside service.'

Suitable, though, as I said. Somehow funerals held in bright sunshine always strike me as a little out of order, although they're the kind we mostly have in sunny Queensland.

My attention began to stray and I only half heard the minister explaining in a kindly drone that Bob had brought nothing into the world and obviously wasn't taking anything out of it. Nothing except his findings on Darkwater and maybe the secret of his death, a small voice whispered in my mind.

I looked around at the assembled crowd. I like the Toowong cemetery, although some think it's an eyesore and ought to be closed. Like a little township, it spills down its hillside, with streets and trees and concrete graves set like beds into the slope, where the dead can sleep in comfort with birdsong over them, undisturbed except for the traffic rushing down the steep roads on either side. There are tall, baroque monuments, family vaults like small stone houses with ironwork gates, and the graves date back into history.

'*Man that is born of a woman has but a short time to live and is full of misery,*' the minister informed us sadly. If that's the official view, no wonder people are leaving the churches. Sounds like a certain ex-Prime Minister who was supposed to have said life wasn't meant to be easy. Where's the hope for any of us? Al Wang says we make our own road, bitter or sweet, from our expectations of life. It works for me.

My eyes caught a movement at the back of the gathering and I watched idly. There was a large grave monument with a spire that soared heavenwards, adorned with angels pointing the way for the soul's benefit, the relatives' hope of better things to come. Behind it, half hidden, standing in the light rain was a tall, strongly built man in a stockman's coat. His Akubra kept the rain off his face, but his long, black bush of a beard glistened with drops. He had moved slightly, but now stood as still as a grave marker, his eyes fastened to mine.

His dark skin proclaimed his race although, once again, his face was mostly hidden so I had no clear idea of what he looked like. I began to feel that odd, hair-raising sensation at the back of my neck that I'd last experienced at Darkwater and, with a rising anger, began to inch away from Joss, keeping my eyes on my watcher.

'Where are you going?' Joss hissed and caught at my arm. 'It's not finished yet.'

'That bloke over there—the aboriginal by the angel monument. He's the same man who was watching the flats last night.'

'Where?' She looked in the direction I was indicating with my chin. 'I don't see anyone.'

'Bloody hell! He's done it again!' There was no one in sight who resembled the figure and I turned around to scan the silent people.

'Micky!' Joss spat. 'For goodness sake, shut up and stay put!'

I wasn't going to make a total berk of myself by charging through the crowd, sliding around in the wet, trying to pursue a man who appeared and vanished like a bloody phantom. I shut up and stayed put, but my eyes were everywhere, looking for just a glimpse of a stockman's coat or wide bush hat.

We were chanting the Lord's prayer. Within minutes the rite would be over, ceremony satisfied, duty done. The air was warm and heavy to breathe, the wind gusted over the hillside, scattering rain, pulling umbrellas askew, and my skin was prickling, not just from the day's warmth.

'. . . and the fellowship of the Holy Ghost, be with us all evermore. Amen.'

Joanna threw a bunch of flowers on to the coffin which was now deep in its final resting place and the minister took her hand and spoke comfortingly to her.

'Come with me,' Joss said suddenly, and began to pull me through the departing people. With a shock I realized she was heading for Joanna. Joanna caught sight of her and her head went up, facing the danger.

Joss stopped in front of Joanna and just stood there. The two women looked at each other in silence, then Joss said all in a rush, 'Joanna, I'm sorry, I really am.'

Joanna gave her the frozen look. 'Sorry?' she said, and she forced the word out.

'Not for being with Bob,' Joss said passionately, 'but that he's dead and that you're hurting.'

Joanna's eyes flashed. 'What would you know about it?' she said savagely, for all her voice was so quiet.

Joss looked startled. 'How could I not know?' she said. 'I don't have him now, either.'

Joanna gave a sort of strangled gasp and turned on her heel to her friends who had been listening silently. I put my arm around Joss and led her away.

David Reeves's red thatch was still visible above the few remaining heads.

'Micky!' He came over. 'Call me, we'll have a beer.' It wasn't an invitation.

'I will,' I promised. 'Come on, Joss, let's get you home.'

I made Joss lie down when I got her back to the flat and gave her a strong coffee, heavily laced with brandy. Purely medicinal. The rain thundered on the roof and she lay, white-faced and silent, as I pottered about, my mind fully occupied with a man in a long leather coat. When I checked again, she was asleep.

I was restless, I tried to work on the book, but gave it up in disgust. Carnie asked to go out and I walked down the stairs with her. The house was deserted, the stairs and passages dark, the air heavy. I carried Carnie out and watched her scrabbling up the wet earth, thinking of Su-lin and her apparent adoption of me. I wondered what Laney had done for Eileen Forrest which she couldn't speak of and a ghost from Darkwater walked over my grave.

'This is bloody ridiculous,' I told Carnie severely, as we went back up to No. 5. 'I've finished with Darkwater. Bob was wrong, that's all.' Carnie looked up at me with unblinking green eyes.

'What would you make of Darkwater?' I asked her. 'You're supposed to be psychic, according to Eileen Forrest. Would you think anything was wrong there?'

For answer, she scratched impatiently at the door and I let her in, made sure that Joss was still asleep, left a note and went out again.

I walked hard and fast, trying to shake off a feeling of depression. Cars went by, tyres swishing, leaving spreading wakes behind them. The gutters were streams. Pretty when the rain first began, with the oil from the roads running in swirling taffeta patterns; now just wet and gurgling. I cast them a black look and turned the corner to trudge the three dripping blocks up the hill to the main road shops.

Paddington is built in the hills immediately west of the city and the main road winds up and around the hilltops, leaving side roads to plunge steeply down on either side, some winding sharply, some just roller-coastering straight down. Houses do the best they can—bless the high stump method which allowed our early folk to build on any angle. On the main road the buildings are low at the front—ground level, but cling with impossibly high stumps at the back to crazy steep slopes, verandahs at all levels and narrow, steep stairs accessing yards of three or four terraces. A nightmare for a lawnmower. I paused a block from the main road outside the *Paddington News* office, a small, turn-of-the-century worker's cottage converted to business premises, as so many of the local firms have done. The windows were cluttered with notices, from 'Give Away Kittens—Last Chance—Mother Going Out of Business' to 'Flat For Rent—Suit Single Working Girl', interspersed with cuttings from the *Padding-*

ton News. I thought compassionately of Joss, sleeping a heart-weary sleep in my bed.

I turned the corner and found myself in the main shopping area, outside my favourite coffee shop. There were a few patrons who had braved the weather chatting over cups of Amanda's excellent coffee, both inside the café and outside where white metal lacework tables were set under a sheltering canopy, overlooking the passing parade. I ran up the shallow steps to shelter, shook my umbrella, and was about to enter the shop when a breathless voice called softly, 'Micky, yoo-hoo, over here!' and I swung around to find Margaret Hill sitting alone at one of the outdoor tables.

'Margaret.' I smiled at her. 'Nice to see you again.'

'Do join me,' she offered. 'I just had to get away for a while. This weather, so *oppressive*, and makes one so very restless, if you know what I mean, and Eileen is so . . . well, poor dear, I'm sure she doesn't mean to be—but it's *worrying*, all the same.'

I hooked my umbrella over the back of a chair and went to see Amanda, returning in a few minutes with coffee and one of the café's famous cheesecakes.

'What's wrong with Mrs Forrest?' I asked.

Margaret sighed. 'I don't really know, but she's been very, well, abrupt and—and *impatient* since you came to see us. She seems to have something on her mind, but she won't talk about it, and she always tells me everything whenever she's upset—after all, I'm almost *family*. And now she's gone out in this rain to work in the garden; I told her she'd catch her death, but she just snapped at me and told me to go for a walk and get out of the house for a while, as if it was *me* who was behaving oddly. I *worry* about her, Micky. She bottles things up inside her and won't confide in me. I'm her oldest friend, so you'd think—but, if you ask me, Mr Slater's accident has got her all stirred up, thinking about how William . . .' She stopped and put her hand to her mouth, looking dismayed.

'It's all right, Margaret,' I soothed. 'I know how her son died, and then her husband. She must have been devastated.'

'That's right.' Margaret leaned forward earnestly. 'She doesn't say much, but she *feels* things. She wouldn't have either William's or Clifford's names mentioned and she was in a queer mood for a long time afterwards. Like she is now.'

'So she works it off in the garden,' I said sympathetically. 'I thought you must have a gardener to keep that place in order.'

'Oh, we do, that's right. But Eileen likes to potter, you know, and she knows all about plants. She used to make her own medicines—potions, I called them. Eucalyptus oil for colds; and tea tree oil, that's good for all sorts of things. She doesn't do any of that these days, though. She had a little laboratory, but she gave all her equipment away years ago, after an accident.'

'Margaret—' I leaned closer to her. 'Tell me about the night Bob had his accident. It's just that, well, I was a friend of his and it would be a comfort to hear about his last hours alive.'

I wondered if I'd laid it on too thick, but she patted my hand comfortingly.

'Oh, Micky, I know. You'd *want* to hear about it. Well, you know he'd been doing the article, of course, and he'd been out to the house several times. He rang quite early on Monday. I was surprised, because I thought he'd finished the interviews and didn't need to come back. But later Eileen told me to make dinner for three, as Mr Slater would be joining us. I wasn't very happy about it, because Eileen had spent quite a long time working in the garden and looked tired, so I made her lie down for a couple of hours. She said he was bringing the finished article to show her and she'd invited him for a meal. She seemed quite excited in her own way, in spite of being tired.'

'I wondered if Bob had been drinking,' I said tentatively, 'and if that might have caused the accident.'

'Oh no, I don't think so. Well, you know, just the normal amount. Eileen likes wine with her dinner, but Mr Slater only had one glass—he said that was his limit. I'm positive he wasn't *affected* in any way at all.'

'And did he show you the article?' If he did, I thought, where the bloody hell is it?

'No, but I could see he was very happy with it. When he arrived he was sort of, well, pleased with himself; keyed up, as if he knew he'd done something we'd be excited about. He didn't show us then, though. And after dinner Eileen took him into her private study and I wasn't invited.' Her face dropped. 'I was a little hurt, I don't mind admitting, when Eileen asked me to bring coffee and not disturb them, but then I thought: Oh well, it *is* her house and history, after all, and she *deserves* to be the first one to hear it. I would read it in the paper in due course.'

'Did you see Bob leave?'

'No. I cleared away the dishes and went to my room to read for a while. I heard him leave, though, and Eileen go to her room.' She shook her head sadly. 'And then, unknown to any of us, he went straight from Darkwater to his death. No wonder Eileen has turned in on herself again. *So* like William.'

'Tell me about Bill's death,' I prompted, hoping she wouldn't remember her friend's injunction.

'We prefer to call him William,' she reproved me. 'Bill is so common, and of course William is the family name. It was *awful*,' she continued, her eyes fixed earnestly on mine. 'William had been having a row with his father, although I don't know what it was about, but he'd told Eileen a few days before he was killed. I wasn't living there, of course; I only moved in with Eileen after Clifford's death. But I was visiting the day before William's accident. Eileen had been pruning things in the garden. She always works outside when she needs to think, and I remember she'd been cutting the oleanders back, out by the old well. She didn't say much, only that William and his father were having a fight and she'd talk to William—he'd listen to her. I wasn't sure, because William clashed with Eileen too from time to time; but she said it was important for the family and William would have to see reason.'

'Were you there the next day, when they had the row?'

'Oh no, but little Debbie told me about it. She was the girl who used to help with the cleaning. A nice little girl. I was sorry to see her go, because she was a very hard worker and loyal, and *obedient*. Very different from girls today.'

I drained my cup, to discover the coffee had gone stone cold while we were talking. Margaret agreed to seconds and I signalled Amanda who, plump, pretty and with her infectious gurgling laugh, was doing the rounds of the tables, wiping them down, socializing with her customers.

'What did Debbie tell you?' I asked.

Margaret stirred uncomfortably. 'It was very disturbing,' she said. 'Apparently William arrived in a real *mood* and Eileen tried to talk to him. She took him into her room and they had a chat but he still went and had a shouting match with his father, then rushed out of the house and took off in his MG—*far* too fast for the weather and the condition of the roads. And so he died,' she finished simply. 'Eileen was very distressed.'

'Do you remember what day that was?' I tried to sound casual.

'The 17th,' she said promptly. 'April, 1973. I remember, because so much happened at that time. First poor William, then Debbie getting the sack, then Clifford's tragic death.'

'Why did Debbie get the sack, do you know?'

'She smashed a *priceless* vase. Of course, with the house in an uproar and everyone so upset and nervy it was hardly surprising, but Eileen was furious. A piece of Darkwater history, you know, and Debbie said she didn't do it, which

made Eileen even more angry. She could never stand servants being untruthful or sly in any way. So Debbie left in
tears. I was very sorry for her. It proved to me how shattered
Eileen really was, to fly off the handle like that. She is always
so much in control.'

'It must have been a trying time for everyone,' I agreed.

'Oh yes, with William and Clifford fighting, then the
police coming about the accident, and Debbie, and Clifford's
death after the funeral, and then those *nasty* rumours.' She
suddenly looked uncomfortable and rushed on quickly, 'It
was very hard for Eileen. I moved to Darkwater a month
later to keep her company. I've been there ever since. I've
no family of my own now, so Darkwater *is* my home, and
Eileen my family. I'd do anything to help Eileen.' She
swallowed the last of her coffee and smiled at me. 'Well,
Micky, it's done me good to get out of the house for a while
and talk to you.' She fumbled in her bag for her purse.

'No, no, let me.' I helped her with her raincoat and we
shook hands as she twittered her thanks. I watched her
pause apprehensively at the bottom of the steps that led
down to the footpath, and then she jerked her umbrella
open and hurried off into the rain, heading for the taxi rank.

What rumours? I wondered. Would she have told me?
Probably not, she shut up very quickly. I didn't want to
push her too far—I might need her to tell me more. I'll bet
John Curtis would know, though.

'Bloody weather!' Amanda paused at my table, collecting
the money I'd left on the bill. 'Stay and have another inside,
and talk to me.'

'Sorry, love.' I pecked her cheek and armed myself with
my own umbrella. 'Things to do, people to see.'

CHAPTER 13

I had practically to bribe the attendant in the newspaper building to let me look at the files of back issues.

'We'll be closing in twenty minutes,' he complained.

'I know exactly what I want—it won't take five minutes.'

'Well, you'd better be right, mate, because we're closing in twenty minutes.'

He looked ominously at his watch, then at the clock on the wall to check the synchronization, and left me to it.

The article about William Trent's death didn't command much space, the papers of the day being all taken up with the latest Government scandal. Shonky land deals, Government ministers bribed, conflict of interests, Opposition calling for an inquiry, that sort of thing; par for the course for us Queenslanders. If he hadn't been the son of Clifford Trent, QC, he'd have hardly rated a mention. But the family was influential, Darkwater was always news and Trent was one of our top barristers. So there it was, just as I'd heard it. Domestic row, driving too fast, wet roads, angry driver, all equalling fatal accident, tragic loss, eminent family asks for donations to charity rather than floral tributes.

The evening paper carried much the same information but mentioned that the autopsy revealed no suspicious circumstances and carried on to complain about the state of Brisbane roads, calling for clearer warnings for dangerous areas and better street lighting.

I flicked through the next day's editions, but already Trent Junior was stale news. Now it wasn't just the land deals, it was an Opposition member naming no sources, but accusing a minister of being involved in certain criminal activities involving laundering money through the purchase and sale of land, tax evasion and putting companies in his wife's name. Like I said, we're used to it. It doesn't raise an indignant eyebrow any more.

A few days later and the Government scandals were pushed briefly off the front page as Queenslanders were shocked to hear of the tragic death of one of this state's distinguished legal minds, Mr Clifford Trent, QC, by his own hand, while in a state of depression following the sad loss of his son. Trent had been named as the man chosen to lead an inquiry into the allegations which had recently rocked the Government. It was also rumoured that Trent would have been mentioned in the New Year's Honours list, almost certainly to be given a knighthood.

I skimmed on to the afternoon's paper. Sergeant David Reeves of Homicide was investigating the death of Mr Clifford Trent, QC, after questions had been raised as to the possibility of murder, following Trent's appointment as head of a Commission into Government corruption. Aha! I thought, nasty rumours, I'll bet. The Opposition was screaming 'Cover-up!'

Keys jangled behind me. 'It's time I was closing,' the attendant informed me triumphantly. 'You said five minutes.'

'And you said twenty.' I glanced at the clock.

'It's near enough to the hour. Come on, mate, this isn't the only room I've got to lock up.'

I let him have his way. I hate to deprive a man of his one moment of pleasure in an otherwise bleak day, and after all, I'd had eighteen minutes out of the wet, out of hearing of the wet, out of sight of the wet. I was refreshed!

After the day's downpour, the afternoon was definitely cooler and the air lighter to breathe. The glowering sky had retreated a few miles up and the rain was only a slight spit. I found a phone-box and dialled.

'How about that beer?' I asked the Inspector.

'Right! Name the pub and I'll be there.'

We took our drinks into the lounge which was steadily filling with tired and damp workers, getting together with their mates for a drink before taking to the glistening wet streets.

'Cheers!' David drank deeply. 'OK, Micky, let's have it!'

I looked my surprise.

'Don't act the innocent with me,' my companion told me. 'What's all this about Bob's death not being kosher?'

'You told me there were no suspicious circumstances,' I reminded him.

'Yes, well, that was before you rang. Don't be a cowboy with this one, Micky, tell the nice policeman all about it.'

'There's nothing to tell,' I countered. 'Really, I don't know what you want.'

His eyes twinkled suddenly and he played with his glass, turning it round and round.

'You're up to something,' he said at last. 'I can feel it. I know you, Micky. Why did you give me the third degree about Bob? Was he drunk, was his car sound, was he on drugs? You said you had a feeling. That means you've heard, or seen, something you probably don't even realize, and you're worried it wasn't the way it looked. So, I want to know, why?'

'Not your case.' I was stubborn. 'You're Homicide, not Accident.'

'I can make it my case, soon enough.' He looked at me seriously. 'No bull now, Micky, what's up?'

'David, I just don't know,' I said awkwardly. 'It's not right, that's all. Listen, Bob was working on a story . . .'

I talked on, mostly to myself. When I'd finished, David got us another round and leaned back in his chair, watching me intently.

'So what you're saying is, because you're not keen on Eileen Forrest, because of a cryptic message on Bob's pad and the coincidence of William Trent's death, in the same place, because of a couple of skid marks on the road, because Eileen Forrest's acting jumpy and Bob's notes have disappeared—have I covered everything? Because of all this, you think—what? Bob was murdered?'

There was a long silence. Finally I shook my head and grinned.

'Sounds bloody silly, doesn't it?' I said ruefully.

'Very bloody silly, if it wasn't for just two things. Bob was ex-crime. He knew his job, knew people, was damned good. All the instincts of a good cop. And, you're being watched, as you know.'

I was startled. 'Yes, I knew. How did you?'

'For God's sake, Micky, I was there today, remember? I heard what you said to Miss Bates.'

'That's why you wanted to see me.'

'Bloody oath! If you're going to start playing games again, I want to know about it.'

'Well, I'm not,' I said flatly. 'I've finished with Darkwater. You were right, David. Bob swerved to miss a possum, Eileen is upset because it reminded her of Bill's death, then her husband's. Bob got it wrong about that note he left, and I've finished the article now, so there's the end to it. I've got a book to write and my life to run.'

'And where were you today?' he asked quietly, but with a knowing grin.

'At the newspaper building. Just interested. I was looking up the pieces on William Trent's death.' He looked smug. 'All right, how did you know?'

'You've got newspaper ink up your arm,' he pointed out. 'I'm a detective. So you're finished with it, are you?'

I acknowledged the hit. 'But what the hell can I do, anyway?'

'Nothing,' he agreed. 'Keep out of trouble. Look, I remember the case with the Trents.'

I nodded. 'Your name was in the paper.'

'Yes, I was put in charge of the investigation. There was a theory he might have been silenced over the Commission into Government scandals, but I couldn't prove it. It was suicide, as far as I was concerned. But, put it another way. Trent has a row with his father. In those days, young William was studying law. It might have been a family matter, it might not. Supposing the son had been got at in some way and asked to try and stop his father taking the job at the inquiry? His father turns him down, and William slams out of the house and is killed, presumably an accident, then Clifford dies, presumably suicide, though some thought not. Next, Bob Slater, in the middle of a story about the family, finds out something, writes his little clue, and dies, presumably accidentally. Now tell me, aren't there rather a lot of deaths around the Forrests suddenly?'

'There've always been a lot of deaths around the bloody Forrests,' I said, and gave him the list as I knew it. 'John Curtis, you met him at the funeral, is a local historian, and he says they're either very unlucky, or cursed. All I know is, the house has the oddest feeling to it. Makes your hackles rise.'

He looked interested. 'What, fear? Unrest? Anger?'

I stirred uncomfortably. 'If I had to name it I'd say evil.' I grimaced as he raised his unruly auburn brows. 'I know, it's an old-fashioned term, but it's all I've got.'

'Evil,' he repeated, thoughtfully.

'So what do you do about evil?' I asked, joking to hide my embarrassment. 'Does the police force have a formula for eradicating it?'

He grinned back. 'The Church would be your best bet. That's their province. The ancients believed fire was the best antidote. The cleansing flame. That's why they sent so many poor deluded women to death at the stake for witchcraft.' He suddenly became serious.

'Micky, take it easy on this one. I don't say I believe a word of what you've told me, but I'm going to make a few very low-key inquiries of my own, along right channels. Meanwhile, get about your business, don't try to be a detective, and watch out for yourself. I'm going to have Harry Andrews look out for that bloke who's been following you and find out why. Don't you tackle him, if you see him again. You're not up to his weight. Ring me, or Harry.' He put down his glass and rose to leave. 'And Micky, don't be a bloody hero.'

'No fear,' I promised him. 'Heroes end up dead too often for my peace of mind.'

I stopped at Luigi's on the way home and bought a takeaway pizza for dinner. I didn't feel like cooking, and I'd bet Joss didn't, either.

She and Carnie were curled up together on the sofa watching TV when I got home. I divided the pizza and joined them. There was a mention of Bob's funeral—he was still a respected journalist—and a picture of the mourners which flashed by too quickly for me to look for the man in the coat. Then the sports news came on, mainly racing, and we turned it off.

'I went back to the office and put the paper to bed,' Joss said. 'Your article will be out tomorrow.'

'So what was all that with Joanna?' I asked, through a mouthful of mozzarella.

'Oh, Micky, I couldn't help it. I felt so sorry for her suddenly, really I did. It can't be easy for her, especially to admit Bob was with me all those years. You know, I think I had the best of the deal, and the best of Bob.'

'And what about some tangible evidence?' I reminded her. 'The photograph?'

'Oh well, I've got my memories, and they're a darn sight happier than Joanna's. I'll do all right.'

I poured her a glass of claret. 'You're a hell of a girl, Joss,' I told her, and quoted, "Here's looking at you, kid."'

She pushed her plate aside, her face pale. 'That's what Bob used to say,' she said quietly.

'Oh, Joss!' I felt helpless to comfort her, but put my glass down and moved closer, putting my arm around her. To my surprise she pressed against me and looked up fiercely.

'Micky, don't let me sleep alone tonight, I couldn't stand it. I need you to be with me.'

With cupped hands she pulled my face towards hers. Carnie was between us and uttered a wail of protest, but we hardly noticed as she pushed her way between us and slid to the floor in disgust.

Loving Joss was so familiar, and yet as exciting as the very first time. Finally we both slept, exhausted, twined around each other.

Some time after midnight the phone rang. I tried to ignore it, but Joss began to stir, so I disentangled myself and padded sleepily downstairs. Carnie's green eyes glinted as I snapped on the desktop reading lamp.

The voice at the other end was deep and mellow, slightly husky.

'You Michael Douglas?'

The rain falling steadily on the roof made it hard to hear. I cupped my hand around the mouthpiece.

'Yeah, who the hell is this? Do you know what time it is?'

'I know.'

'Well, what in God's name do you want?'

There was an amused tone in the soft, deep voice.

'It isn't what I want, mate, it's what you want.'

'What the—what are you on about?' I was feeling justifiably irritable. 'What do I want?'

Joss said in a sleep-drowned voice, 'Micky?'

The voice on the line chuckled. 'Deathwater, mate. You want to know about Deathwater.'

CHAPTER 14

I jerked awake. 'What do you know about Deathwater?'

The deep, rich chuckle came again. 'I know everything about it, mate.'

'And you'll tell me?'

'Maybe. Depends, doesn't it?'

'On what?'

'On how I bloody feel about it, mate. But I'll talk to you, no sweat.'

'When?'

He paused and I could hear the same heavy rain at his end.

'Tomorrow. Botanical Gardens, Mount Coot-tha. Ten o'clock.'

'Whereabout in the Gardens? How will I know you?'

'Don't worry, mate, I'll find you—and you'll know me, all right.'

'I'll be there.' A faint memory of David Reeves's warning floated across my mind, but I forgot to listen. I was too busy throwing caution to the winds.

I didn't tell Joss. She'd have wanted to come too and, for all I knew, I was setting myself up for something nasty. But the cautious little voice in me was drowned out by a sudden, urgent need to find out for once and for all what disturbed me so much about Darkwater, who my mysterious caller was and, in spite of my protestations, which William was on Bob's mind when he doodled his last message.

But don't get me wrong, I'm no hero. I'd go to the Gardens all right, but with both eyes well open and my back protected as much as I was able. After all, I reasoned feebly, nothing much could happen in the Botanical Gardens, in the full public eye.

Next morning in the car park by the Planetarium I wasn't so sure. Of course it was raining, not much, just a steady drizzle, but banking black clouds and a leaden sky spoke of more thunderstorms sweeping in from our pet depression in the east. Although the usual tourist buses were pulled up, there were very few souls abroad, and I suspected most of the tourists were in the retaurant passing the time either eating or buying toy koalas and tea-towels from the tourist shop. Would someone brave the wet to come to my aid if I called? Probably not.

The air was damp but quite fresh as I made my decision and left the car. The only good thing about this weather, I thought sourly, is that the Capri is permanently washed. It stood lightly on its tyres, its long sporty lines making it look eager to dash away; my only refuge in a hostile green wilderness.

'Where the bloody hell am I supposed to go?' I thought crossly. I wasn't really worried, but it was a pretty stupid way to arrange to meet someone. It was just before ten. I couldn't stand about like a fool in the car park, so I picked any direction and began to walk slowly along the pebbled path towards the herb garden. Here, borders of peppermint, sage and thyme massed fragrantly, their subtle scents mingling with the damp earth smell. I realized nervously that the place was almost deserted and the winding paths which disappeared mysteriously around clumps of wet vegetation created too many hidden corners for my comfort.

There was a continuous sound of running water, not just from the rain-fed rivulets running down the paths and diverted into channels which plunged steeply down in places to disappear through the greenery; but mainly from the artificial waterfalls and bubbling creeks which fell in a series of rapids to spill over stone slab causeways. Ponds, swollen from the constant rain, enjoyed the attentions of a multitude of exotic-looking ducks and other water birds.

My path looked like losing itself again and, not wishing

to be quite so private, I glanced once more over my shoulder and turned off, following the signposts to the tropical dome. There was shelter there, although it was the last place I'd want to enter. The dome lifts its geodesic head above the Gardens, an acrylic bubble criss-crossed by an aluminium frame. It's supposed to be a controlled atmosphere for the benefit of the exotic and fragile plants within its confines— to me, it's a nightmare. Rare plants may like an over-hot, close, airless atmosphere. It makes me feel claustrophobic and a little panicky as I fight for breath. It's one place I stay out of when I go to the Gardens. But underneath the horrible affair is an open, walk-through shelter, which houses cacti on one side and bromeliads on the other; a nice, dry, desert place, with interesting spiky, fluffy, and well-fleshed inhabitants growing peacefully behind their protective wire barriers. Here I'd be out of the rain, I'd be able to see clearly who was coming in from both sides, and I'd bet there'd be various other people sheltering there as well, among the friendly little cactus plants. My mysterious night caller could find me there, or forget it!

The musky scent of Indian figs hung in the air, thick and sweet. A group of camera-hung Japanese tourists from one of the coaches chattered ahead of me, laughing and posing, each one desperate to be in the photograph as well as taking it. Difficult! I grinned in reply as they hailed me, and willingly put off the evil hour ahead as I herded them together with smiles and bows and gestures, balanced my umbrella over my shoulder, and snapped the photo. We gesticulated, bowed, laughed and parted, and they moved off in the direction of our latest acquisition, the Japanese Garden, once set up at Expo 88, now relocated in the Botanical Gardens, a gift from the Japanese Government. And very nice, too. I was left more alone than ever, after the bright little encounter.

As I neared the dome the sky let go and, with a bright flash of lightning, began to dump its load, angry bullets of rain firing down, pelting my umbrella with noise, sending a spray up from the path as the rain rebounded fiercely. I began to run towards the building ahead, when a hand came from behind, clapped me on the shoulder, nearly frightening me into a coronary, and turned me towards the doors of the dome, and a husky voice said, 'In here, mate.'

In the deluge, I was torn between dropping dead with shock and getting out of the rain. The latter won and I obeyed the strong clasp on my arm and ran, side by side with my bearded companion in the stockman's coat. He pushed open the doors and we entered the hot, sterile atmosphere together.

As always, my heart pounded in alarm at being caught in the dome trap. I pulled the heavy air into my lungs, feeling the familiar claustrophobic band tightening around my head. My companion shook the water from his wide-brimmed Akubra and gave me a slow grin.

'G'day, mate.'

'It's you!' I exploded, angry now as the fear of the unknown subsided. 'Bloody hell! What do you mean, watching my flat, turning up at the funeral and keeping me under observation?'

His dark, liquid eyes gleamed with humour. 'Had to be sure, mate. Had to know. Maybe you're safe to talk to, maybe not, see? I gotta make up my mind about that. The name's Jimmy, Jimmy Crane.'

He held out his hand and I gripped it automatically. 'Well, what's all the mystery? Why couldn't you simply state your business over the phone?'

He shook his head, his beard glistening with a spray of rain. 'I gotta wait. Check you out some more. You do it my way and you'll find out everything you want to know— maybe.' He looked around. The dome was deserted. 'We can talk in here. Come on, up the top.'

'Do we have to?' I muttered, but followed him as he led

the way up the stairs which flanked a deep, opaque green pool in which were submerged stands of water plants. My head was beginning to throb. The steps led up to a circular path which ran around the top of the dome, between the pool in the middle and a continuous bed of plants and ferns around the clear acrylic walls. A fine spray of water from pipes along the walls kept the plants moist and the air unbreathably heavy. I tried to concentrate.

'We can see from here if anyone comes in,' Jimmy said calmly, pointing to the doors below. The rain drummed mercilessly on the clear dome, hemming me in even more.

I faced my companion, forcing back the urge to get out of the sickly hot atmosphere into the clean fresh air. 'What do you want?' I managed.

'I got a story to tell,' the big aboriginal said quietly. 'You wrote a piece on Deathwater for Bob. Bob was a mate of mine.'

I was about to ask him how he knew I'd taken over the story, then remembered it had been published in this morning's *News*. In my excitement I jumped ahead of him eagerly. 'Do you know what he found out? About the death of one of the Williams?'

'Maybe.' Jimmy Crane was non-committal. 'There's a lot of Williams. Maybe I know about all of 'em. But why should I tell you?'

'You rang me,' I reminded him tartly.

'Yeah!' He sighed. 'And I don't know about you yet. You're a friend of one of those coppers who came when old Trent died. The big red-haired bloke. Said it was suicide. Now he's an Inspector. Maybe you're OK. I don't know. You don't keep good company, mate.'

I was stung by the implication. 'Reeves is OK, he's a good cop and a mate.'

'If you say so.'

'Why do you call it Deathwater?' I asked urgently. 'I've tried to find out, but everyone has a different story.'

He looked at me for a moment, then turned to gaze into the pale green water at his feet.

'My people call it Deathwater. Because of William. Because of what he did in the beginning.'

I frowned. 'The first William? The founder? I was told there was a tribe nearby but he ran them off.'

Jimmy Crane snorted angrily. 'He never ran them off, mate, he bloody wiped them out. My people. It was their sacred place, their Dreaming. He killed them all.'

I was startled. 'My God, how?'

He looked awkward and pulled at his beard. 'White fella's ways. It's taboo,' he said at last. 'My people can't speak of their dead. Maybe you'll find out later. But after—that—the black fellas called it Deathwater. And it will be until—well, until it changes.'

'What will change it?' I asked curiously.

'I can't tell you. Maybe later, not now.'

'I want to know. Perhaps I can help.' I held his eyes with mine. I didn't know what I could do, but in his face was a terrible sadness which overwhelmed me. He seemed to hesitate and I took my chance.

'Tell me about your people, the ones at Dar—Deathwater. Were they part of the Turribal tribe?'

He grinned faintly. 'You got that from John Curtis? He says you're OK, maybe he's right.'

'You know Curtis?' I asked unnecessarily.

'He told me to talk to you. OK, I'll take a chance on you. Maybe I'm a bloody drongo, but you look all right.' He paused, organizing his thoughts. In the close heat my head pounded and the sweat beaded my forehead and trickled down my back. He seemed unaffected by the atmosphere and began to speak slowly, choosing his words.

'My people were Turribal. Here before the white man came. We were all one people but lived separate, you know?'

I nodded. 'John told me.'

'Yeah! My people lived on the place where Deathwater

is now. We had fresh water in the spring, our sacred place was nearby, our ancestors' place. Part of our Dreaming. We couldn't leave, see? We had to keep the sacred place or our Dreaming would be finished.'

I nodded again. The Dreamtime is the aboriginal concept of the creation, when the ancestor spirits made all the people and animals and painted themselves on rocks and cave walls. I knew each tribe also had its 'Dreaming', or myth that explained the origins of the tribe and was handed down in secret ceremonies. It's vital to the tribes to remember their Dreaming and maintain the paintings, or their essence, their *raison d'être*, is gone forever. Then I had a sudden thought.

'You say "my" people, but that can't be right. You said William killed all the Darkwater people and the historical records say that the Brisbane aboriginals had died out by 1860.'

His dark eyes glowed with a hundred painful memories.

'Don't you believe it, mate. Maybe the white fellas think that. They don't know everything.'

I was surprised. 'Are you saying some of the people survived?'

'I'm telling you my story, that's all. You believe what you like. Believe your white fella history books.'

I was silent, waiting.

'I told you, we couldn't leave. Some of the whites weren't too bad. But Forrest was a bastard, see? He wanted all the land, even the sacred place, although he was frightened, too. My people, they fought back. He was a strong man, but superstitious. Scared of the bush and the black fella, scared of our magic. He drove us away, we came back. So he thought he'd finish us off, for once and for all. And he did to us what you call genocide. He took our land and thought that was the end of it. All my people gone, no one to fight him any more.'

'Hang on a minute,' I challenged him again. 'How can

they be your people? That means they can't all have been killed.'

A little, knowing smile flickered in his beard for a moment. 'Maybe some escaped,' he said in his deep, quiet drawl. 'Who knows? But if they did, and your history books got it wrong, maybe they moved away into the hills and waited, near Deathwater.'

'Why did they do that?'

'The sacred place has to be looked after. The elders keep it fresh and strong and the Dreaming is safe.'

'But surely there aren't any aboriginals at Darkwater now.' I was becoming more and more inquisitive about this strangely authoritative man with his dark skin and gentle, gleaming eyes. I felt, in his own deliberate way, he was going to unravel the mystery for me, if he thought he could trust his secrets to me.

'Don't you believe it, mate. There's always a black fella at Deathwater, always will be, until things're put right. They don't know, the Forrests. It's not their land. Never has been. They don't belong there and they know it. That's why they're afraid. They fenced off the sacred place, fenced it and grew a hedge to keep the spirits out, killed all the snakes, but they couldn't fight the black fella's magic.'

'They can't have killed all the snakes,' I said idly. 'I saw a snake at Darkwater, in the servants' quarters; or maybe it was a spirit snake,' I joked. 'It disappeared quickly enough.' I stopped suddenly. Jimmy Crane was staring at me as if he'd seen William Forrest's ghost. Shock and disbelief vied for attention on his expressive face.

'You saw a snake?' he said, barely above a whisper. 'You'd better tell me, mate.'

I explained the incident, puzzled at his reaction. 'Later, even though Mrs Forrest was so adamant about it, I thought it over and I know I was right. A dark, banded snake, about so long.' I measured with my hands.

He shook his head slowly. 'Curtis was right about you,'

he said at last. 'Forrests, they're dead scared of snakes, no sweat. They don't understand. Think they're evil. Kill 'em all, whenever they see one. White man's rubbish, that. That snake you saw, he's not evil. I know him. He's a good spirit, that one. He's watching you, taking care of you. Deathwater's a bad place. That snake, he looks at you and keeps you safe there. But he's warning you too. He's saying, "You keep the law here, or you be in big trouble, mate." But he let you go safely, so he knows you're OK.'

I digested this in silence, watching the submerged plants, feeling my skin prickle, the hairs rising slowly on the back of my neck, the heat draining my energy.

'Mrs Forrest said there were no snakes at Darkwater,' I said, forcing back the nausea which threatened to engulf me. The heat and closeness were almost unbearable now.

He grinned. 'They know they're watching them, looking at them. They know about the spirit snake, the ancestor of my people. They know about the Dreaming. They got a reason to be shit-scared.'

'Why?' I insisted.

He looked me full in the eyes, his face suddenly expressionless, carved out of dark granite.

'When William Forrest did—that—to my people, they put a curse on Deathwater.' His voice was cold and deliberate. 'The curse is on all the Deathwater Forrests. They won't have any good there, bad spirits take them all, their family is filled with fear and hate and evil thoughts. And we wait. We wait until the end. Not long coming now. And the Forrests will give back what they stole. Deathwater they made it, Deathwater it's been for them. You wait, Micky, one day, you'll see.'

CHAPTER 15

The doors to the tropical dome opened abruptly and my Japanese tourists spilled in on the lower floor, giggling and shaking out their wet raincoats, snapping their umbrellas shut, holding up their cameras. They peered through the viewing window at the bottom of the pool, interestedly searching the thick, warm, green water. A couple saw me and called out, pointing. I waved back but said urgently to Jimmy, 'I've got to get out of here, mate.'

His story had held at bay my feeling of sick apprehension for as long as it could. Now the airless atmosphere was pressing in on me and breathing came harder every second.

He followed me as I blundered down the stairs, under a fine mist spray, and out of the doors. I dragged in gulps of cool, damp air and tried to look nonchalant as my panic subsided.

Jimmy eyed me inquiringly. 'You don't like it in there?' he asked with mild surprise.

'Not much. It's a bit hard to breathe,' I understated wildly, feeling like an idiot, my head splitting. 'Let's get out of this rain.' I walked quickly around the corner, into the shelter of the cactus garden. Surprisingly, there was no one else there.

'This is better. We can talk here. Is that OK with you?' I turned, but Jimmy Crane was gone. I was alone, talking to myself.

'Damn!' I swore. 'I wanted to know more about the Forrest deaths. He knows what Bob knew, I'm sure of it.'

I ran back into the rain, but there was no sign of Jimmy. Once again he'd just melted away.

As soon as I arrived home, I phoned John Curtis.

'Save the Paddington water tower,' he intoned. 'Oh, Micky! What can I do for you?'

'I spoke to Jimmy Crane today,' I said bluntly.

'Oh, good, I suggested he look you up. He knows a lot about Darkwater. I hope you didn't mind, but I see you've already done the article, so I suppose it's too late. Never mind. How did you get on?'

I hesitated. 'He's an interesting bloke, but a bit secretive. He comes and goes a bit abruptly.'

He chuckled. 'He has to feel comfortable with you before he'll tell you anything.'

'Well, he did tell me about the aboriginals at Darkwater, but he took himself off just when I thought he was warming up.'

'He'll probably make contact again. If I see him, I'll tell him you want to hear more. We'll be turning you into another historian if you're not careful. Bloody good article, I thought.'

'Thanks. It's an interesting place,' I said non-committally. 'Did you know Crane was a friend of Bob Slater?'

'Yes, I rather gathered there was a connection. Well, let me know if I can do anything else for you.'

I poured myself a cold lime juice and sat down to do some serious thinking, going back over my strange conversation with Crane, remembering he'd first said William Forrest had somehow wiped out all the Darkwater tribe, then intimated that some had escaped and still watched over their land. Was that possible? I wondered just how effective an aboriginal curse could be, thinking of all those deaths in the family, and remembered stories of bone-pointing and medicine men running silently through the night in feathered shoes so as not to leave a print, and the dark and secret rituals where tribal law was passed down to the young men in bora ceremonies. I knew some aboriginal magic was powerful and totally effective; for instance, I knew blacks could be 'sung to death'; but surely you had to believe before it worked, and it was a matter of psychology. You believed, so you died.

But supposing you were given a helping hand? William Senior had been seen apparently talking to himself; but what if the maid had got it wrong and there had been someone else there? Someone whose hand had pulled the trigger, someone who had silently melted into the bush, as Jimmy Crane melted out of sight? And supposing Crane was not content to let the ancient curse do its work and had pushed things along a little? Could he have caused the deaths of Clifford Trent and his son? It was hard to tell his age, but I was sure he'd have been old enough sixteen years ago to be able to organize a little vengeance for his murdered people. He'd easily remembered David Reeves's investigation, and somehow got the idea that David was—what? Corrupt? Because he'd agreed to the verdict of suicide. I didn't know about that, but I'd be willing to stake my life on David's honesty. But Jimmy's? I knew nothing about him. Perhaps it was passed down with the tribal law. Wipe out the Forrests, make them pay, get our land back. Then I remembered his sad, dark, gentle eyes and shook myself impatiently. Was that the face of a ruthless killer? I couldn't believe it. He was as fanatical in his own way as Eileen Forrest was in hers, I was sure, but . . .

Anyway, Bob Slater wasn't a Forrest and he was a friend of Crane's, so that rather discounted his death. God, it must have been an accident, and what was I doing trying to prove anything else?

I tore my mind away, but it came as reluctantly as Carnie from a saucer of tinned milk. I uncovered my neglected manuscript and forced myself to the typewriter.

Ten minutes later I had the Yellow Pages in hand and was running through the listings for nurseries. It was there, Green Fingers Nursery, proprietors Charlotte and Colin

Dysart, the address out of town where there was space to spread out and grow plants.

Lunch first, I decided, and Carnie agreed. Her enforced imprisonment in the flat was making her bored and hungry.

'Never mind, love,' I soothed her. 'It will stop raining eventually—I hope!'

The Green Fingers Nursery, bordered with graceful jacarandas and poincianas, lushly green in the rain, covered its land in neatly divided plots and greenhouses with Sarlon cloth covers, plants tidily together in their species and types, ticketed and catalogued and tamed. By the entrance was a long shed-cum-shop, open down one side, with a counter at the back. It was crammed with earthenware and plastic pots in an array of sizes and colours, shelves of books on every aspect of landscaping, gardening, mulching and growing every type of flora. A selection of kitsch garden ornaments spilled out into the wet and racks of little pot plants and seedlings and catalogues blocked the way to the counter. Bundles of stakes, tools, and sacks of fertilizers, manures and top soils were stacked against the back wall. A warm, musty scent of compost, damp earth and green growing things permeated the place.

I sidled cautiously around the various stands, praying nothing would collapse, smash or get caught in my shirt. As I approached the back of the shop, an attractive, deep-tanned woman in her late forties, with thick, dark salt-and-pepper hair cut in a once again fashionable 'thirties bob, and a gentle face with rather dreamy grey eyes, popped up from behind the counter and smiled warmly at me.

'Can I help you?'

'Well, yes.' I spread my hands helplessly. 'I want to send a pot plant to my aunt. Don't know a thing about plants. Can you suggest something?' Adrian, my mind said, she's not one of your William Forrests, she's the dead spit of dreamy old never-belonged-here Adrian.

'Would you like to come through into the nursery? We

can pick something out.' She threw a large black mac over her jeans and man's khaki shirt and indicated the way. I hoisted my umbrella and followed.

'Pesky weather,' she complained. 'We're beginning to lose quite a bit of stock. Lucky Colin built an excellent drainage system. Other nurseries on the flat, like us, are getting flooded out. We'll do another week, but then God help us!'

The rain pattered and splashed on my umbrella. Across the beds a broad-set man in shorts, naked to the waist and sun-bronzed, worked in the drizzle.

'My husband,' she said with a wave in his direction. 'He finds it easier just to get wet than keep putting on a mac, which tends to wrap itself around you and get in the way. Now,' she continued, 'we've got some lovely plants at very reasonable prices. Come into the greenhouse.'

In the warm green atmosphere I was uncomfortably reminded of the dome in the Botanical Gardens. Repressing a shudder, I pretended interest in the variety of orchids, indoor plants from bushy to vine trailing, and a selection of bonsais. Finally, my mind still at Mount Coot-tha, I chose an attractive bromeliad, cousin to the pineapple, with its similar spiky leaves and little pink face peering through its water cup.

'Good choice,' Charlotte said briskly. 'I'm particularly fond of the broms. Now, do you want us to deliver?'

'Please.' We picked our damp way through the gardens back to the shelter of the shed. I made my move, risking everything on one throw.

'The name's Mrs Melanie Carter-Jones, address . . .' I gave Laney's address and watched hopefully as Charlotte Dysart's hand slowed and she looked at me in astonishment.

'There can't be two,' she laughed, delighted by my feigned puzzled expression. 'You won't believe this, but I know your aunt. Mrs Carter-Jones is a friend of my mother!'

'No!' I prayed I'd gauged my reaction of amused surprise

just right, and shook my head. 'Isn't that just like Brisbane!'

'Of course. A high-rise country town.'

'I'm amazed!' I laughed. 'And I just picked you out of the phone book.' Not really a lie. 'I happened to be coming this way.' Also not really a lie. 'Who is your mother? Maybe I know her.'

'You never know. She lives at Bardon.'

'Oh? I live at Paddington.'

She laughed. 'Then that really is a coincidence. I'll bet you know her place. It's a historical home called Darkwater, at the top of Bardon.'

'This is extraordinary!' Oh God, I'm not overdoing it, am I? Her face was innocent, no suspicion there, and why should there be? 'She must be Mrs Forrest! You really won't believe this, but I met her recently. I did an article on Darkwater for the local paper and was very kindly invited to tea. Not only that, I was telling Laney, my aunt, about it and she was remembering the early days, when she and your mother were young.'

'Oh, that's marvellous!' Charlotte grinned her delight. 'I just have to tell Col. He won't believe it.'

'What won't he believe?' The tall, broad-shouldered man had come in, the damp on his body glistening, his muscles hard and knotted under the dark tan. His greying gold hair was plastered wetly to his scalp.

Charlotte, still thrilled at this example of life's vagaries, explained. He grinned and held out his hand. I gripped it, liking him and the obvious warmth of his personality.

'My name's Douglas,' I told them. 'Micky Douglas.'

'Well, g'day, Micky. Would you believe it? Not a customer in days and then one pops up with family connections.'

'Extraordinary,' I repeated. 'Your mother certainly is a wonderful, strong person,' I told Charlotte.

'Oh, a tartar,' she laughed back. 'Always has been, and definitely supreme head of the Forrests. Rules like a tyrant, but she loves us and only has our good in mind. I drop in once a week or so to make sure she's OK and have a look over the gardens. Darkwater's where I got my love of plants and gardening, Micky. I put myself in charge of the place, as far as the gardens go, and hired and fired the help.'

'The gardens are wonderful,' I said. 'I believe Mrs Forrest's a keen potterer.'

'Oh, Mum's a good amateur botanist.' She pointed to a small booklet on the shelf behind her, *A Guide to Australian Bush Remedies* by Eileen Forrest. 'We still sell her little booklet and it's very popular these days, with so many people getting back to herbal and natural cures. She taught me heaps.'

'Surely you don't still do all that gardening?'

'Oh no, no time, anyway. I got Mum a really good bloke. He used to work for us here, part-time. Of course Mum was dead set against him. She's got certain prejudices and he's an aboriginal. A bloke called Jimmy Crane.'

I heard my voice, 'But surely there aren't any aboriginals at Darkwater,' and Jimmy's firm reply, 'Don't you believe it, mate.'

'However, Jimmy's beaut. I used to kid him that he might be black, but he had green fingers. Mum had to give in. Prejudiced she may be, but she'd let nothing stand in the way of Darkwater's good. So she potters, Jimmy does the hard graft, and I supervise.'

'And the result is superb,' I told her.

The wet on Col was literally steaming in the warmth of the day and the heat of his body after its labours. 'If you're going to talk family, I'll slip out the back and clean up. Micky, you'll have a drink with us, mate?'

'I'll be delighted. But aren't you—er—working?'

Charlotte shrugged. 'This weather's a killer for plants and customers. You make today crowded. We'll put the buzzer on in case someone comes in, and sit out the back. What'll it be, Micky? Coffee? A beer? We've light, if you'd prefer.'

'Thanks, light it is.'

A door at the back of the shop opened into a cosy little two-roomed space, one room for the shower and the other with a sink, small stove, fridge, a cupboard mounted on the wall and a low table with several latticed metal garden chairs around it. Gardening magazines and catalogues were stacked on the table, alongside a murder mystery and a portable radio.

Over the sound of the shower's hiss, Colin Dysart's voice was raised in a deep, melodious rendition of the latest Billy Joel hit. Charlotte grinned and jerked her head in his direction.

'Thinks he's Caruso. But he can certainly hold a tune, which is more than I ever could.' She dispensed the beer in tall, cold glasses which had come out of the fridge with the bottle, and raised hers.

'Cheers. Here's to crime.'

CHAPTER 16

'You're the fan?' I indicated the paperback on the table.

'Yes, but I never get time.' Charlotte shrugged. 'Started that one days ago, and look how far I've got. It's usually the magazines and the job I read about.'

The noise of the shower stopped abruptly and Col switched to a plaintive negro spiritual.

'I'se gwine down Jordan,' he boomed.

'Something to eat, Micky?' Charlotte rummaged in the cupboard and brought out a tin. It was full of shortbread.

'Ah.' I tried a piece. 'This is good. Is it Margaret Hill's?'

'That's right, how did you—oh, of course, you went to tea at Darkwater. Bloody woman's a pain in the neck, but she can certainly cook. Her shortbread melts in your mouth. I got this last week.'

'You don't like her?' Oh god of gossip, if there is one, let's have some idle, revealing chat.

'Can't stand the woman. Never could. So pathetic and always wimping around Mum. She was always in and out of Darkwater, sneaky old thing, pretending to have come just to gossip with Cook, listening to all our secrets on the sly and trying to be Family. She's as addicted to the Forrest legend as Mum is. However, pretend as she may, she's *not* Family,' she said, with a certain satisfaction.

'She seemed very devoted to your mother.'

'Yes, to be fair, she's been a loyal friend to Mum and patient with her. Mum's never suffered fools gladly and she's getting worse as she gets older but, give her her due, the Pill might be a garrulous old fool but she never resents Mum's moods and I've heard Mum be quite sharp with her.'

'The Pill?' I raised an eyebrow.

'Sorry.' She had the grace to blush slightly. 'Forgot you weren't Family. We used to call her that when we were kids, Mrs Pill, or the Pill, instead of Hill. My brother Billy really resented her friendship with Mum and wondered how Mum tolerated her. There's nothing wrong with her,' she added hastily, 'just that she's wet and twittery and over-eager. Billy said she sneaked, and he couldn't stand that.'

'Billy?' I said quietly. 'Didn't he die in some sort of accident?'

'Car smash,' she said shortly. 'Poor Silly Billy. So—alive, and then, in an instant, so very dead. God, I felt that. We were best mates as well as brother and sister. I loved Billy. Wild as they come, lived hard every minute. I suppose he was bound to smash himself up in that bloody MG sooner or later.'

Col joined us in fresh shorts and a T-shirt and poured himself a beer. 'What're we talking about?' he asked. 'Have I missed anything?'

'We seem to have got on to poor Bill,' Charlotte said wistfully and he smiled into her eyes, a warm smile of complete understanding.

'Cheer up, darling, all a long time ago now.'

'Yes.' She shook herself. 'It was a bad time. I suppose you know Dad shot himself over Bill's death?'

'I heard,' I said awkwardly. 'Also that some people thought it was to do with the Royal Commission into Government corruption.'

'Oh, that?' She snorted. 'Bloody rubbish! But in a way that appointment did cost Dad his life. Billy didn't want him to take the job. They'd rowed about it for weeks. A lot of senior politicians, police and judges were very bloody suspect and it could have been the most awful stink. Dad would have really had no authority, but he couldn't see that and wanted to get ahead. The whole thing was a set-up by the Government in order to be seen to be fighting corruption.

A number of very senior ministers were up to their necks. It would have been a toothless, pointless exercise which wouldn't have proved a thing. Billy said any honest cops and pollies wouldn't come forward because it was rigged, and they'd be in all sorts of strife. Poor Billy.' She sighed. 'He had a passion for justice and couldn't tolerate dishonesty or underhandedness. He once dropped his best mate after he'd found him cheating in one of the exams. You should have heard him. He'd have made a great barrister. So he rowed with Dad and slammed out of the house one night and killed himself. God, I wish I'd been home that night. Billy listened to me. I could've talked sense into him, I know it.'

'Your mother tried,' I reminded her. She looked surprised.

'You do know us well, don't you? A fat lot of good Mum would have done. Probably made it worse. Anyway—' she shrugged—'Bill was a wild devil and as stubborn as Mum. Dad was never up to their weight. Like putty in their hands mostly, poor Dad.'

'I loved hearing about the early history of Darkwater,' I said, wanting to change the subject to less painful matters. 'I saw some portraits. You've certainly a family resemblance.'

'Yes, but not The Nose, you'll notice,' she laughed, and rubbed her own neat, straight one. 'I look more like Adrian Forrest, our black, black sheep.'

'I heard about him, and that the two branches of the family never communicate.'

She grinned and looked sideways at Col. 'If Mum had her way it'd be true enough, but actually, Chris and I are good friends. I must have taken after Adrian's side of the family more than they bargained for, because years ago I thought how bloody silly all that was, and that I was missing out on half my relatives. All those cousins out west. So I wrote to Christopher—he's head of the Belgara Forrests— and when he was in Brissy again he looked me up. He's a nice bloke, a straight, practical, slow-talking west Queenslander.

He comes and stays with us when he's down for the Ekka, and on business.'

Of course. All the country folk are in Brisbane in August for the Ekka, the Royal Queensland Exhibition, the annual showing of the best of our primary industries. All the states have their 'Shows'. Sydney's Royal Easter Show is world famous. Christopher Forrest would certainly bring down his best stock and fleeces and be in town for the ten days, doing business.

'Don't you dare tell Mum,' Charlotte laughed in mock horror. 'She'd skin me alive if she knew I talked to "those other Forrests".'

I laughed with her. 'I don't expect I'll be seeing her again. I finished the article. It was published in today's *Paddington News*.'

'Oh, ripper! Can I get a copy? I'd love it.' She grinned wickedly. 'I'll photocopy it and send it to Chris.'

'I'll send you one,' I promised, enjoying her humour and friendliness. A thoroughly nice pair, the Dysarts.

We chattered on through the humid afternoon, the rain an ever-present rattle on the iron roof. It was pleasant and relaxing. When I took my leave they farewelled me, standing in the shelter of the shed, arms around each other. I felt cheered by our meeting and thanked God they didn't seem to suspect my motives.

Al Wang was on his way out as I ran up the stairs to No. 5.

'You have been out laying ghosts?' he asked politely.

'Maybe stirring up new ones.'

'Be careful. Not all the past is dead and gone.'

'Don't I know it!' I pulled a wry face. 'See you, Al.'

He called back an afterthought. 'Your phone has been ringing with great frequency. Someone is very keen to contact you.'

'Oh well, whoever it is will ring again, if it's important.'

Carnie greeted me with a display of affection that could only mean it was time for food. As I opened a can the phone rang again. The voice at the other end was slow and bleary, the product of a dozen too many.

'Gawdstrewth, I've been ringing you all bloody arvo.' The pub sounds in the background made him hard to hear.

'Who is this, please?'

'Never you bloody mind. You're Michael Douglas, wrote that piece in the *Paddington News*? Read it. Read the bit on the other bloke, Slater.' Joss had written a couple of paragraphs about Bob, his work and his unfortunate death, to go with the article.

'That's right. How can I help you?'

His voice staggered and recovered its balance. 'Got something to say. I gotta tell you something. It was bloody awful and I gotta tell you.'

'Tell me what?'

'That night, that bloody night, Monday, I saw him, that's what. Saw the poor bugger.' His words slurred indistinctly. 'Bought it, poor bastard, right into the bloody fence. Drunk as a skunk, he was. Bought it good and proper.'

I gripped the receiver. 'Are you saying you saw the accident? Bob Slater?'

''Course that's what I'm bloody saying. You got a hearing problem? Poor bugger! Bloody rain, and him swerving all over the bloody road. Nearly ran me off the side. Then, crash, poor bastard. In the bloody rain.'

'Look, can I see you? Talk to you?'

'Jesus wept! Just shut up and bloody listen! You can't see me, no way.'

'Why the hell not? You were an eyewitness to a fatal accident. The police know a motorist drove away. They've been calling for you to come forward. Didn't it occur to you to tell them?'

'Gawdstrewth!' It was an indignant yelp. I could hear the panic in his voice. 'You trying to get a man into strife? I can't go to the cops, Jesus bloody wept! They'd bloody get me, fair and square.' He went off into a muted string of drunken obscenities.

'OK, hold on to your hat! Why are you ringing me?'

'Gotta tell someone; you're a mate of the poor bastard, right? Look, I done nothing, but I can't go to the police. But I can't get the frigging thing out of me mind. Honest, mate, it's driving me bloody crazy and I ain't been sober since then. I gotta tell someone. You listen, mate. I'll tell you. Please! You just listen.'

CHAPTER 17

'OK, OK,' I soothed. 'I'm listening. Take it easy and start from the beginning.'

'I'm drunk,' he informed me unnecessarily. 'Swore off the bloody piss after the cops done me for drink-driving. Scared the shit out of me, and lost me licence. Not the first time, see? Drink bloody driving. But I wasn't on the piss on Monday, no bloody fear! I learned me lesson good and proper.' He paused and gathered his thoughts, his breath becoming heavy and laboured. I reached for the message pad and began to scribble notes.

'Is that why you can't go to the police?'

'Yeah, o'course. I was driving without me bloody licence. I was being extra careful, see. They warned me, next time the bloody clink. Boggo Road. Well, I was coming up Kaye Street, nice and easy, bloody rain making the roads a bastard, and this bloody car comes down, weaving all over the bloody road. Frigging headlights going everywhere. Scared the shit out of me. Mad, drunk bugger, I thought, and then he was on top of me. So I sat on the bloody horn and then he saw me and skidded over to his side again, then he lost it completely. I'd pulled up, see, shaking like a bloody leaf, thanking me lucky stars, and I looked back and saw the poor bugger go straight into the bloody fence.' He began to sob, noisy, drunken gasps, and I hung on, just as shaken, waiting for him to recover.

'All right, mate, take it easy. Just tell me.'

'Gotta-tell-someone,' he gasped. 'On me bloody conscience since bloody Monday. Daren't tell the missus, borrowed me mate's car. Daren't tell the cops.'

'What happened after you saw the car crash?'

'Poor bastard,' he sobbed. 'I went back, as you would.

T'see if he was OK. Poor bastard's head all bashed in, blood running everywhere. He looked dead. Thought he'd been killed outright. Jesus bloody wept!' The horror was in his voice as he remembered. 'Wanted to call the cops. Couldn't, see? No—no licence. They'd bloody do me. Nothing I could do for your mate. Dead as a frigging doornail. Blood everywhere. Then over the road lights were going on, people calling out—looking out. I bloody hopped it. Thought no one'd notice me, not with all that going on. Got myself home and didn't sleep a wink. Couldn't stop bloody shaking. Next day I went out and got pissed and I been pissed ever since. Couldn't tell, see. Then I read today the poor bastard was alive and didn't die till later. Oh, Jesus!' He stopped abruptly, and continued to sob quietly.

'Look, will you at least tell me your name?'

It was a bad move. His voice screeched into the phone. 'You frigging mad? Didn'tcha hear a bloody word? Listen, mate, I've told you all I saw and you can tell the cops and maybe I'll sleep now and be able to forget the poor bastard's face. But no names, mate, no frigging pack drill. But it's the frigging truth I've told you.'

'Look, can I just ask you—' But he'd gone. I heard the music and shouts and clatter for a moment and the noise of him fumbling with the phone, then the line was dead.

I leafed anxiously through my scribblings and, ignoring Carnie's wails of protest from the kitchen, rang David Reeves. He listened in silence as I gave him the story and, hearing my distress, went straight to the heart of the matter.

'Micky, this bloke, whoever he was, couldn't have done anything. The people across the road were there in minutes and called the ambulance. Unless he'd been a doctor, the eyewitness couldn't have helped, or got to a phone any quicker. It wouldn't have made a difference to Bob. He'd have died anyway. The surgeons did everything they could, but in a way it was a mercy that he went quickly. His brain was damaged. He was better off going without regaining consciousness.'

'Thanks,' I said after a pause, thinking: Clever Inspector Reeves!

'I want the man, though. He was calling from a pub, you said?'

'Is there any point? He was scared stiff and obviously having a horrendous attack of the guilts. I'd be amazed if he drives again, with or without a licence. I felt sorry for the poor bloke. He hasn't done any harm, you say he couldn't have helped Bob—.'

'Eyewitness to a fatal accident, leaving the scene of an accident, driving without a licence,' David ticked off. 'Failure to report an accident, and claims Slater was drunk when the autopsy says not. We need to get him sober and go through it with him. He could give us valuable information, when his brain dries out. Damn!'

There was a pause. Carnie had given up the kitchen and was rubbing around me. 'Try the Paddington Tavern,' I said reluctantly.

'Oh? Why?'

'He's a local, reads the *Paddington News*. And before he hung up, I heard someone shouting "Lennie". Lennie's a barman at the Tavern.'

'Good man! It won't be us, it's not a homicide—yet. But I'll get a mobile patrol to pick him up and get him into CIB for questioning—after he's sobered up.'

'Get back to me, David.'

'I will, don't worry. But he probably won't be in a fit state to question for some hours, so don't bite your fingernails to the elbow.'

I hung up and was brought back to other priorities by Carnie, who was now taking short runs and bumping her head into my ankles.

'Sorry, love. OK, OK! I'll feed you.' She tripped me up all the way to the kitchen.

While Carnie was contentedly cramming herself and uttering loud, ecstatic purrs, I brewed myself a coffee and sat down to have a hard think. It was long overdue, but I'm not always that logical, tending to follow my feelings. I wanted to know what Bob knew and I wondered, if I followed his clues specifically . . .

Well, Deathwater. Everyone had a different version of how the name had come about, and only two tallied in any way: Laney's idea that it had come from colonial times and Jimmy Crane's assertion that William had wiped out the tribe who used the waterhole. I suppose I'm slow, but suddenly the penny dropped. I'd heard stories of similar incidents, where tribes in the way of the white expansion were destroyed by—That had to be it! My God, no wonder they cursed him and his family for all generations.

How did William really die? I'd already got some way on that. I could discount Mrs Forrest's brother. Laney had heard the story first hand and there'd been plenty of eye-witnesses. He wasn't pushed. I'd probably never find out if William Senior had shot himself or had the job done for him by a vengeful black or anyone else—no doubt he had plenty of enemies—or if he was talking to himself or pleading for his life. Will Junior? A tree could be made to fall anywhere by a skilled axeman, but he was the axeman in this case.

'So, William Trent,' I asked aloud, 'what happened to you that night? And was it the same as Bob, and if so, who did it and how?'

A gust of wind tore savagely against the house, rattling the windows. I looked around uneasily, then, on an impulse, got up, turned all the lights on and the TV.

Flood scenes, accompanied by dramatic music. Reporters under umbrellas and ominous skies. Depression now affecting as far north as Gladstone, as far south as Byron Bay. Bad news for northern New South Wales; several towns on the flats threatened. The familiar Brisbane street names in

low-lying areas, always the first to flood. The infamous
Northey Street, areas of South Brisbane, local creeks spreading, basements flooding, hopeless shrugs of the victims.
Happens every time. Why doesn't the council, the Government, God, do something about the roads, about the drains,
about the bloody weather?

A cheery weather girl with a toothpaste commercial smile
brightly let drop that our own pet depression had joined up
with a mate further up the coast and seaside resorts had
better watch out. She chattered on about troughs and lows
and depressions, and wished us all a beautiful day tomorrow. Some hope!

Joss came in, wet and grumpy, and we cheered ourselves
with food and conversation and watched an old movie about
a lost patrol in the desert. We savoured the couple of hours of
heat and dry, even though the characters were dying of thirst.

'Huh!' Joss snorted. 'Let them come over here. Look,
Micky . . .' We'd turned the TV off and Joss was eyeing
me, embarrassed.

'Say on, love,' I advised her.

'Well, about tonight. Is it all right if we don't, well, what
I'm trying to say is that, last night, I hope you don't think
I was . . .' She tailed off, but I'd got the message.

'It's OK, love, really. Last night was because you were
hurting for Bob, but I know you, Joss. You're not the type
to go from one man to another just like that. You needed
me, I was there, and it was lovely.' I grinned at her, hurt
inside, wanting her. 'But it was only for last night. I didn't
expect to, well, take over from Bob.'

'Oh, Micky.' Her eyes welled with tears and she leaned
towards me and gently kissed my cheek. 'I do love you; but
as friends—you know.'

'Yes, I know. I love you too, Joss.' I smiled at her, trying
to mask my sense of abandonment. I could have used some
comfort tonight. 'You go to bed, love. I'll be sleeping down
here again.'

'Thanks.' She went up the short flight of stairs. 'Good night, then.'

''Night.' I glanced at the clock as I took our supper things through to the kitchen. Only 10.30. As I was stacking the crockery the phone rang.

My nerves stretched. It was too late for a friendly social call. I recognized the husky tones at once.

'Micky? Jimmy Crane.'

'Do you always call in the middle of the night?' I asked irritably, my pulses racing.

'Why not? Night's still a piccaninny, mate. Let's meet.'

'When?'

'What's wrong with now?'

'What's wrong with the morning?'

'Everything.' He chuckled. 'Got something to show you. Been thinking about you. I reckon you might be OK. You want to meet or not?'

'Where?'

'Pick me up outside the Tavern. By the way, there was a bit of a blue here earlier. Cops pulled a drunk geezer. Sobbing in his beer, he was. Made a phone call, real upset, the poor bastard. Then, half an hour later, patrol came and picked him up. Maybe something to do with the phone call, eh?'

'You didn't happen to overhear his conversation—accidentally, of course?'

'I might have, mate, I might have. Well, come on if you're coming.'

The line went dead. I called up to Joss that I had to go out, and left the flat. Carnie's green eyes glinted with interest in the single light on my desk.

CHAPTER 18

Jimmy was waiting for me in the shadows, out of reach of the street lamps, as I pulled up ten minutes later outside the Paddington Tavern. He crowded the passenger seat, smelling of damp warmth and leather and beer, and the stale smoke of the bar.

'Why all this cloak and dagger business?' I asked. 'Why not simply come to the flat?'

He chuckled. 'You got a copper watching you. Watching to see I don't grab you, maybe.' I wondered where he got his information. I'd forgotten David had said he'd detail one of his sergeants, Harry Andrews, to keep an eye on me. A good choice. Harry looks less like a policeman than anyone I can think of.

'How'd you know?'

He grinned at me, but all he said was, 'Just follow Given Terrace up into Latrobe and turn off when I tell you.'

Aha! I thought, Bardon. But I followed his instructions without query.

He guided me through narrow back streets, some overhung with trees so they were more like tunnels, some so narrow two cars would have difficulty passing each other. There was no other traffic in these back lanes and terraces. When he finally signalled me to stop, we were pressed up against a cliff face on our left, and to the right the city lights glowed wetly across the way.

The rain was taking a well-earned breather and the wind had dropped to a whisper as we got out of the car. Jimmy closed his door with barely a sound and motioned me to do the same. There were no houses really close here—the land dropped away to a gully, rough and rocky. A waterfall was leaping noisily down from the run-off which streamed across the road from the cliffs above. I remembered Eileen's description and peered at the rough bush area with its wild native tobacco plants.

'We're underneath Darkwater,' I whispered.

'Too right, mate. Said I got something to show you. Come on.'

I followed his dark figure around the rock face, and he suddenly produced a torch and shone the thin beam into a fissure in the rock which was mostly hidden by dripping bushes. No one passing would ever guess it was there. He moved towards the rock. I figured if it was wide enough to accommodate him, I'd get through easily. He worked his way through, sideways, as if he'd done it forever, and beckoned me. I got wet through as I pushed the greenery aside. The cleft was about seven feet high, narrowing uncomfortably at the top, and maybe seven or eight feet long. I pulled myself thankfully through, to stand under an overhang of rock. In the dark bush something rustled, disturbed by our presence.

'Snakes?' I asked in an anxious whisper.

'Possum.' His reply was low and matter of fact. 'Snakes, they won't worry you, no sweat. You're with me. But don't come down here alone, or that spirit, he'll forget he looked after you before.' He gave the ghost of a chuckle.

'What did you want to show me?'

'This!' He shone the torch upwards and I drew an astonished breath. For the overhang created a shallow rock cave, sheltered from the wet, and the walls were covered in a mass of primitive art, painted in red and yellow and black ochres; symbols and circles, hand prints, strange beings with large heads and obvious male attributes, animals of all sorts, wallabies, possums, and dingoes, all highly stylized, with their patterned bodies showing the internal organs. On one wall a large banded snake undulated in its ochre skin.

I expelled my breath slowly as the beam of light played around the ancient art gallery. Jimmy Crane squatted on the ground, watching me, half solemn, half amused at my wonder.

'Bloody hell!' I managed at last. In this tiny stand of natural bush time had gone back a thousand, ten thousand years. 'What's all this about?'

Jimmy motioned me to join him and I adopted his easy, squatting position. His guttural tones deepened and it was as if we were in some distant, isolated, vast bush, rather than cheek by jowl with a large, modern city.

'This is the place of my ancestors.' I could hardly see his face in the darkness, the only light now coming from the city lights reflected in the low-hung cloud. His eyes were dark hollows. 'In the Dreaming, the ancestor spirits, they made this place. All this land is part of our Dreaming, ancestor spirits live here. This is our sacred place, where the law was passed on. There's power in this place. Maybe you feel it, too.' I couldn't speak, but my senses were all awry. His low voice, almost a chant, continued.

'This bush, and Deathwater land, all part of this special spirit place. Everything's part of it. The trees and the rocks, they belong together. This is a place of initiation on the Dreaming Track. Ancestor spirits, they painted themselves on the rocks in the Dreamtime, and the tribal elders, they've got to keep the sacred places and show respect for the ancestor spirits, so we come back and renew the paintings to keep the Dreaming strong and keep our bond with the land.'

I interrupted him. 'Are you an elder?'

'Yeah. I'm an elder of the Turribal.'

'What does it mean, the Dreaming Track?'

I saw his bulk shift and he stood up, huge against the light cloud sky. I thought he was going to refuse to tell me, but he squatted back down and I sensed his grin.

'I gone so far, eh! Might as well tell you. You bloody white fella, but you got the spirit protection. OK. During the bora ceremony, when the young boys get initiated, they

go from the tribal place, the first bora ring, and then go
with the elders, away from the women, to the secret ring.
They get painted with red ochre and do a special ceremony.
Then they get led along the Dreaming Track to each sacred
place. All these places are connected by the Track and all
get visited in right order. At each place they do ceremonies
and learn sacred songs and dancing and each place is a
speaking place.'

Close to us a night bird flapped on heavy wings through
the little piece of dripping bush and a shrill scream shocked
the darkness as some animal met its fate.

'Mopoke,' Jimmy said calmly. 'She's getting her dinner,
bush rat.' He nearly had to scrape me off the overhang.
Slowly my heart came back to normal as I listened to his
voice, undisturbed, continue its husky tale.

'Speaking place, that's a spirit place where they get told
a little bit more of the law and the Dreaming. They get
special powers, they learn the law which says how we live
together, respect each other, about our mother the land,
and the ancestor spirits. They learn all things are bound
together, all part of the one. They get told, respect the land
our mother, respect the plants, the rocks, the birds, fish,
animals, trees. All are part of the Dreaming. They learn all
secret and sacred things and when they return they don't
come back as boys any more. Now they're men and they
live and hunt with the men. They know the law and the
elders guard the law.'

He was silent at last and I felt the enormous power of the
man and this place. It was as if, through some magic of his,
I could feel my own links with all the life around me; the
bush, the rocks with their ancient paintings, the hunting
owl, the sure-footed possum. And his sadness affected me
deeply. Here was something vast and ancient that touched
me to my deepest level of pain, overwhelmed my senses and
cast me adrift from all my modern lifelines. My voice seemed
to come from a long way away, from someone else.

'William Forrest, he poisoned the waterhole, didn't he? And your people drank the water and died. That's why it was called Deathwater.'

He stirred and his head turned slowly. 'How'd you figure that?'

'I've heard of similar cases out west, where the whites poisoned the blacks' water supply so they could move on to their land.'

His sigh was deep. 'Not all died. A party was out hunting. Came back, found the others. I can't talk about that, mate.'

'I know, it's all right. The bastard! Do you know how he died?'

'Shot himself.'

'Or was shot—maybe by a Turribal?'

'Could be. I wasn't there, mate. Curse got him. Good riddance.'

'The curse could've been helped along.'

'Could have. I wouldn't know.'

I bet you do, I thought. I bet you know every bloody detail about the Forrests. Handed down from father to son, I don't doubt.

'Did the curse get his son, or was that helped along as well?'

'Tree fell on him, I heard. Tree spirit got him.'

'Explain,' I said. 'Please, Jimmy, it's important.'

'You got a lot of sense for a white fella. A lot of understanding. I'll tell you, but I can't make you believe it.'

'Try me.'

'OK.'

A damp breeze stirred the dark night and water sprinkled from the greenery in little showers. Jimmy paused, then spoke. 'That tree was special. One of the speaking places, up there.' He pointed up the natural gully, towards Darkwater. 'William, he knew. First we tried to live in peace. Told him where the sacred places were so he could keep the law. He turned it against us. Caught some of the tribe taking stuff from the garden.'

'I know,' I said. 'Curtis told me. He hanged them from a tree on his own property.'

'He hanged them from the ancestor tree, the sacred place.' The deep voice was harsh. 'He violated our sacred place.'

I couldn't say anything. The deliberate profaning of the aboriginals' religious place horrified me.

Jimmy's voice was low and savage. 'He never forgot it. It never let him rest. He was dead scared of that tree from then on. Tree spirit powerful and vengeful, make no mistake. When his son came back, he'd had enough. Ordered him to cut down the tree. He was too shit-scared to do it himself. So the tree killed his son. Fell the wrong way. What you might call an accident.'

'Bloody hell! You're not serious!'

'I'm dead serious. Up till then there was a track from Deathwater down here. Forrests, they used to bring their friends down to the sacred place, the white bastards. But after the tree killed William's son, they all got very scared of the ancestor spirits. They put up a big fence, grew a big hedge, to keep the spirits away.'

A thought struck me. 'The riding accident, the Forrest children, when John was killed.'

He'd stood up again, silhouetted against the bush and sky. I joined him, stiff after squatting for so long. The night was cool and the bush scented.

'You're pretty smart,' he said quietly.

'William said he saw an aboriginal, but Adrian saw a snake. What was that all about?'

'Adrian was a friend, even then. You know about Adrian?'

I nodded. 'John Curtis told me.'

'Even when he was a boy, he respected the law. He knew the bush, knew the belonging. He saw a snake spirit, I reckon. Under snake protection, same as you, Micky. Maybe one of my people was there, maybe William made it up.

But good spirits protect those who keep the law, black or white.'

He stepped out of the shelter of the overhanging cliff and inhaled the dampness that was drifting in. 'Come on, mate. More rain coming.'

'Damn!' I followed him out. 'Wait a minute, Jimmy. You didn't tell me you were the gardener at Darkwater.'

His teeth gleamed for an instant. 'You didn't tell me you wrote kids' books!' he retorted.

'I want to get into the house by myself. Is there ever a time when both ladies are out?'

'Yeah.' He didn't ask me why. 'I'll call you when the coast's clear and you can come up.'

'Thanks. It'd better be soon.'

He swore softly. 'That's the trouble with you bloody white fellas. You're always in such a bloody hurry.'

CHAPTER 19

Jimmy wouldn't come back with me. I got the feeling he wanted to stay with his ancestor spirits for a while, so I left him there beside the road, his dark bulk blending with the bush. He muttered something about having something else I'd find interesting and he'd maybe show me next time, and stood watching as I started the Capri and pulled away. I drove back under the low, luminous clouds, deep in thought, still stirred by the experience of the fantastic cave so secretly hidden under the Deathwater—Darkwater—cliffs. I shook myself. He'd got me doing it, now. Eileen Forrest hadn't told me about that cave.

'And she'd not be likely to,' I told myself, 'if she believes in the curse. It was her father who fenced off the gully, after William Junior died.'

I let myself quietly back into the flat. It was strangely silent without the constant drumming of the rain. I pulled the curtains back. The swollen clouds hung, almost touchable. They still had a lot to contribute to our misery. I scowled up at them.

Joss's breathing came deep and regular. She was well into dreamland. I'd have followed her example, but my mind was racing, my senses alert, my nerves taut, still under the influence of Jimmy's spell, feeling all the hurt and horror of a long-gone time. I quietly poured myself a drink and settled down at my desk, deep in thought, just the desk lamp for company until Carnie, curious as ever, joined me, sitting on the desk, patting at my hand with a comforting paw.

'Hello, love,' I told her softly. 'Well, sweetheart, I reckon there's something very sussy happening up at Darkwater, don't you?'

She gave an encouraging purr, so I continued to talk to

her and she listened to my low voice, ears on the twitch.

'I'm going to find out a few things.' I ran them by her and she seemed to approve. 'D'you reckon Su-Lin and the snake spirit'll watch out for me again?'

She gave me a candid look that said, 'Frankly, Micky, I don't give a damn,' yawned widely and began to wash herself.

By the time dawn drizzled in I was asleep and didn't stir, even when Joss packed her things, wrote a note, left it propped up against the coffee-pot and left the flat.

'Micky,' Joss had written, in her abrupt way. 'It occurred to me after you left last night that I wasn't being very fair on you, staying here. So I phoned Felicity, and she'll put me up until I can get home. Thanks for all you've done, looking after me, and caring. I'll call you later—and I'm OK, really. Love, Joss.'

My pyjamas were neatly folded on the bed, my dressing-gown hanging, my bathroom tidied and wholly mine. I sighed and made breakfast.

Thinking over my conversation with Carnie in the wee small hours, I mapped out a plan of campaign. I was considering my first move when Laney rang.

'Darling boy, thank you,' she said. 'What a dear little plant.'

'You're welcome,' I said. 'I'm surprised they'd deliver on a Sunday.'

'Charlotte brought it. Said she was passing this way. I think she was interested to see how I'd weathered. She told me about the extraordinary coincidence, you just happening to drop in, and being my nephew.'

It was hard to read her tone of voice. 'Ah!' I said awkwardly. 'Well, love . . .'

'I had a long chat with her.' Laney overrode my hesitation. 'She told me all about your visit—and your conversation.'

'Did she? Well . . .'

'I was curious myself,' Laney swept on inexorably. 'Stirred up all those memories; so I gave Eileen a call.' Innocence dripped down the phone.

I drew a deep breath. '*Did* you?' I said politely.

'We had a lovely long chat about the old days. She was surprised to hear we were related. She said your article was excellent and what a nice boy you were.'

I nodded to myself. 'Thanks, Laney.'

'My pleasure, darling. Thank *you* again for this little bromeliad. Take care of yourself.'

'You can depend on it,' I promised grimly.

Why my family ever called her Looney Laney, I'll never know. The woman's got a mind like a steel trap.

Next to call, as I was about to escort Carnie downstairs, was David Reeves.

'Micky? Well, we got your eyewitness. Bloke called Bluey Linden. He's sober, more or less, considering he's been tying one on since Monday night. Incidentally, it cleared up a missing persons. He hasn't been home for a couple of days, or at work. His wife reported him missing yesterday, after checking with all his friends. She's hopping mad. What we do to him won't hurt half as much as when he gets home.'

'Did he help?'

'No, pretty well gave us the same story he told you. He couldn't remember much more. Oh well, a policeman's lot and all that. It was worth a try.'

'Will he go to gaol?' I was concerned.

'That's up to the magistrate. The man has a record of drink-driving and this time he deliberately chose to drive without a licence. He'll hardly get off lightly. Some people never learn.'

'Well, thanks for letting me know. I feel guilty, wrecking your Sunday.'

He chuckled. 'Don't tell me you think it's all down to you. I had to work today, anyway. Micky Douglas's problems aren't the only ones on our plate, you know.'

I grinned, relieved. 'By the way, you can call Harry off. My watcher's a friend.'

'He made contact?'

'Yes, I met him yesterday.' David swore. 'Don't worry, I wasn't taking any risks.' I know that now, I thought grimly, but I wasn't too bloody sure yesterday afternoon.

'You won't be told, will you? So what's his story?'

'Oh, he just heard I'd wanted some information about Darkwater for the article,' I said airily. 'He's the gardener up there. Of course it was too late, the story's been published, but we met and had a chat. He's OK.'

'I'm glad to hear it, although I'm not sure I believe a word of it.' David's voice was dry. 'Anything else you haven't mentioned?'

I hesitated. 'I found out Mrs Forrest's daughter, Charlotte, has a nursery. The Green Fingers, down on the south side. I—er—dropped in for a chat.' I heard David's smothered exclamation. 'Nothing in-depth, David, just a friendly chat. She confirmed what you thought, that Bill Trent and his father rowed about the Commission, but not because Bill had been got at. Just the opposite. Apparently he was absolutely honest and thought the whole inquiry was a set-up by top judges, police and ministers to stop the truth coming out. Of course, with the Fitzgerald Inquiry bringing all the corruption into the open, we know how much of that sort of thing did go on, so he was probably right. He didn't want his old man involved in a cover-up. Clifford Trent apparently thought he could do some good if he went ahead.'

'I see.' There was a pause, and I thought he was going to say something but he brought the conversation to a close and hung up.

Following my own line of thought, I rang John Curtis.

'The maid?' he asked. 'Oh, little Debbie. Hang on, let me think. Debbie Harris, that was it. She was only about sixteen or seventeen, so she'd be—what? in her mid-thirties now? No, I don't know what happened to her. Is it important?'

'Oh no, just curious about something someone said.'

'Well, not a problem. If I hear anything about her I'll let you know.'

'Thanks.' I wondered if he knew about the ancient treasure in aboriginal history underneath Darkwater's back fence, but held my tongue. If Jimmy wanted him to know, no doubt he'd tell him.

Heart beating a little faster, I rang Charlotte Dysart.

'Thanks for dropping Laney's plant over so quickly.'

'It was lovely to see her again.'

'Charlotte . . .' I hoped she was as nice as I'd thought, or I was in big trouble, but I couldn't get any further without her and there were some things I badly wanted to know.

'I'm still here,' she said, after a pause.

'Sorry. Look, can I come and see you? It's about Darkwater.'

'Of course! You'll be welcome any time. Come over for lunch.'

I demurred, but she insisted. 'If just a scratch salad and bread on a plate on your knees will do.'

'Lovely!'

The rain was sheeting down as I got to the nursery. Col Dysart was nowhere to be seen.

'He's at home, catching up on the paperwork, it's so slack here. We do turn and turn about.' She smiled at me and deftly disposed of my umbrella where it would cause the least wet. 'I thought last night it might've stopped raining at last, but I guess not.'

A damp breeze gusted a mist of water into the open-fronted shop, but only the plants were in its path. Charlotte beckoned me into the back room where she'd arranged a delicious-looking meal on the small table. The various magazines had been stacked on the floor.

She poured a beer for me—she was already half way through one. 'Cheers!' She raised her glass. 'Now, Micky, what's all this about?'

'It's about you being very kind and forgiving me,' I said slowly. She raised her eyebrows, but said nothing. I continued, hoping to hell I was doing the right thing, knowing she'd have every right to sling me out on my ear. 'I wasn't absolutely honest with you yesterday. I wasn't just passing, and it wasn't a coincidence. I'm sorry, Charlotte, but I knew you were Eileen Forrest's daughter and I wanted to see you—to find out what you were like.'

Her expression didn't change. She just kept looking at me with a faintly questioning lift to her brows, her face serene. 'That was a bit of an elaborate way to go about it,' she said at last.

'Yes—but it wasn't just idle curiosity. I need your help.'

She shrugged. 'And I suppose all that about an article was a fabrication too?'

'No, no, of course not. I brought you a copy.' I handed the sheet over to her.

'Eat!' she commanded, waving at the food. She sounded as imperious as her mother. I began to eat nervously as she read the story and accompanying tribute to Bob.

'You're very good,' she said. 'Mrs Carter-Jones tells me you're an author.' She laid the paper down. 'Well, you haven't done anything to upset me as far as I know, just been a bit devious, so I'll withhold my judgement. Presumably you're here to explain why the hoax?'

'It's about your brother, Bill,' I said gently. 'It's possible he was killed in some way—murdered, I mean, but I can't prove it and I don't mean to hurt you or stir up bad memories.' I watched her face carefully. 'I just want the truth, and I think you cared for him enough to want to help me.'

She'd been looking down in a non-seeing way at the table. Finally, she raised her eyes. I was surprised to see only a gleam of humour in their grey depths.

'I'm not upset,' she said, sensing my concern. 'It's just not exactly a new thought, that's all. Of course, with all the row over the Commission, then Dad's death, the whole thing was reinvestigated. How can you hope to prove anything when all the experts failed?'

'Because I think it's happened again,' I said, and watched her surprise. 'I think the truth, whatever it was, is still being hushed up and, until I find out what the hell's going on, it may not be the end of the deaths associated with Darkwater.'

Her intelligent eyes went back to the paper. 'This man, Bob Slater. Is it him you mean?'

'Yes. Let me explain.'

She picked up her plate and began to eat, watching me closely between mouthfuls.

'I'm listening.'

CHAPTER 20

I told Charlotte about Bob, his cryptic doodling, how I'd narrowed it down in my mind to Bill Trent.

'I think that Bill might have been put out of the way because he tried to stop your father heading the inquiry, and because he knew it was a whitewash. If he'd threatened to expose all he knew—he had the influence, the right connections—an accusation by the son of Clifford Trent would have carried a lot of weight. Suppose someone very high up was threatened? He might have gone to any lengths to stop the truth coming out. Your father, not believing Bill, might have mentioned it to some judge, or minister—'

'And then what?' She shook her head. 'We know the car wasn't tampered with. Bill wasn't drunk.'

'What if that was wrong? Reports falsified?' I said urgently. 'Look at all the appalling things that are coming out in the Fitzgerald Inquiry. Any corrupt police—senior officers—could have a report tampered with. Look, I know David Reeves, the man who investigated your father's death, and—'

She cut in quickly. 'A tall, red-haired man? Don't tell me you suspect him? He was nice, a lot better than the one who came first. Sergeant Reeves took up the case later on.'

I chuckled. 'He is nice and, no, I don't suspect him, but I think *he* might suspect things were hushed up. He's a friend of mine and I'd vouch for his honesty any day. After Bob's death, so similar in every respect, I happen to know he's making fresh inquiries, very low-key. He's an Inspector now, so he has more clout. You see, there was an eyewitness to Bob's accident. Said he was drunk, swerving all over the road. But the accident report said he wasn't above the limit. How do you explain that?'

Charlotte just looked shaken. 'For God's sake, Micky!' She picked up her glass, drained it and poured another, her hands trembling. 'You said you wanted my help. How?'

'I want to know exactly what happened on the night Bill died. I want to talk to someone who was in the house. So far, all I've heard are second-hand reports.'

'But it's so long ago, who'd remember all the details? And would you get the police to listen? I mean, you think they mucked about with the evidence anyway.'

'I don't even know if there's anything to find. I just want to be absolutely sure I've covered everything. Call it a feeling, that's all. You had a maid, Debbie Harris. She seems to have been a witness. Do you know what happened to her?'

'Little Debbie?' She thought for a moment. 'Wait a sec, she came from a domestic service—Handy Help, that's right. We always got our staff from there. They had good, trustworthy people. If they're still operating, they may know.'

'Right, thanks. Now, can you tell me about Bill's funeral?'

It took her by surprise. 'Bill's? Why?' she asked blankly.

'Because that's when your father died, and some didn't think it was suicide. Supposing Bill had been eliminated, to stop him talking, and your father had told someone— perhaps the wrong someone? There must have been a few powerful Government people around, at the house? I'd like to know if anyone could have slipped away from the group, perhaps killed him, and then come back unnoticed.'

'Good grief!' Her face was pale, her eyes dark grey smudges. 'Let me think . . .' She frowned in concentration. 'Of course there was a crowd at the funeral, courtesy to Dad, but afterwards, just the family—servants, Margaret, Sir Martin White, who was the head of Bill's chambers, John Curtis, a few of Dad's closest colleagues; the Deputy Premier came briefly, but didn't stay too long. And most of the guests were gone before Dad went to lie down. He was

looking bloody awful and Mum told him to have a rest
before dinner. He said he would, but asked us if we'd all
wait because afterwards he had something he wanted to tell
us.'

'Then what happened?'

'Well—' her eyes searched back into the past—'we all
sat about, chatting. Margaret went to make us some tea, I
think, because Cook was so busy. Mum went outside into
the garden to get away from everyone, the side garden with
the travellers' palms. I don't remember—oh yes, Sir Martin
went out to see if Mum needed anything.'

'Then? When you heard the shot?'

Remembering was hard for her and she shivered slightly,
but her voice remained steady.

'We were startled, of course. Everyone leaped up and
started talking at once, trying to work out if it really was a
shot, and where it had come from. Margaret came rushing
back from the kitchen, practically in a state of shock, and
went twittering on like a maniac. Sir Martin—I think he
came in then, said Mum hadn't needed him and he'd gone
for a walk. He came in through the front door. I could see
the entrance. Then Mum came in, looking like death but
very calm, and said, "That was a gunshot. I must see if
Clifford is all right," as if she *knew*. It was so eerie, because
everyone hushed up and just stared at her. She went to
Dad's room and we all followed her, and, and . . .' She
covered her face with her hands.

'It's OK, Charlotte,' I said uncomfortably. 'Look, don't
go on if it's too much.'

She looked up, her eyes very dark, but dry. 'No, it's all
right. I—I haven't talked about it since then. Mum forbade
us to mention it or Dad's name again, so—so we didn't, out
of respect for her feelings. Perhaps we should have got
together and talked it out. I'm sure a psychologist would
have recommended that—get it out in the open, talk about
our feelings and let it go.' She gave me a half-smile. 'This'll

be good for me.' She went to the small fridge, opened a fresh bottle and poured us another beer. I've never been a big beer drinker, although bending the elbow's supposed to be our national sport, but now I was grateful for the cool, refreshing liquid which was calming to the nerves. She went on.

'He did it with one of William's guns, you know, the first William. It hung on the wall in William's study. He must have taken it on his way to his bedroom, or gone back when he decided to—well, that's what we thought,' she finished miserably.

'Or someone else took it,' I countered, watching her. 'Now, that points to someone with intimate knowledge of the house, and presumably the gun wasn't loaded, so someone would have to know how to load an old-fashioned gun. I certainly don't, and I expect most people wouldn't have a clue.'

She looked sober. 'I do,' she said. 'All the family do, and the ammunition is kept in William's study, too, just where he kept it. All the family knew about it. Oh hell!' She pulled a tissue out of her pocket and blew her nose. 'The Christmas before, Dad and Bill got into an argument about guns. They were both keen marksmen. They'd argue about anything at the drop of a hat. Began this fight about the accuracy of old guns compared to modern ones. They set up a target in the garden and got a couple of William's guns and we all got involved. Mum knows all about everything to do with the old days. Because she's the "keeper of the history", so to speak, she had to give permission for us to use the guns and she showed us all how to load them, except Dad and Bill already knew. A boring business, when you think how easy modern guns are.'

'Who was there?' I asked, trying to mask my excitement.

'Oh, me, Col, of course, Bill and Dad, John Curtis had dropped in for drinks, Margaret—except she was nervous of the guns, jumped when they were fired, and generally

made a fuss. Mum was there, and my two. I've got two
children, Margaret and William—carrying on the tradition,
as you see, but we call Margaret "Maggie", to avoid confusion, and William's always been "The Kid", from Billy
the Kid. He was addicted to cowboy movies. They were
only young then. Let me think.' She screwed up her face,
concentrating.

'We got Cook to come and watch, but she didn't want
anything to do with "all that nonsense" and she was busy,
as usual, so she left after a few minutes. Oh, and my sister
Amelia and her husband, Brad, had come over from the
States, and their kids, Jamie and little Brad. Amelia was
pregnant and feeling the heat very much, so she didn't join
in. She stayed mostly under a tree in a hammock.'

'So that was all? Jimmy Crane wasn't there?'

'Oh no, it was Christmas. Jimmy was working at Darkwater but he was away, presumably with his family.'

'He has family?' I asked, intrigued.

'Well, I assume so. Somewhere in northern New South
Wales—cousins, or something. Lismore way, as far as I can
remember.'

'So it turns out that all the family know how to load and
use the guns,' I said slowly.

'That's crazy!' Her voice was sharp. 'Who on earth in the
family would've—' Then she gasped. 'Oh Lord, I just
remembered. It was one of the guns we used that Christmas.
Of course, all this came out during Sergeant Reeves's investigation. We'd all handled the guns, but there weren't any
fingerprints, only Dad's, because naturally they were all
very well cleaned and dusted every week.' She shrugged.
'Micky, the gun was in Dad's hand and only his fingerprints
were on it.'

'Anyone who reads detective stories has seen that done,'
I objected, and she nodded unhappily.

'But—oh, I just can't imagine anyone in the family—oh,
it's impossible!'

We finished eating in silence and she gathered our plates and stacked them in the little sink. 'Micky, let me find out about Debbie for you,' she said suddenly. 'I can do it far more easily, as she used to be in our employ. I'll ring you if I can find out where she is now.'

I accepted gratefully and took my leave. 'Oh, and before I forget, have you got a book on natural poisons? Plants, and that sort of thing? It's for my landlady,' I lied hastily. 'This wet's bringing all the bugs out and she wants to get away from chemical sprays and try some environmentally safe things.'

'Good for her.' Charlotte rummaged around and brought out a paperback.

'This'll be what she wants. Explains how to mix and use the poisons safely, and has a section on repellents that don't actually kill, but discourage—pennyroyal, garlic, that sort of thing.'

I paid for the book and drove off, my mind working through all she'd told me. As I entered 18 Princess Road, Monica opened her door, waving the *Sunday Mail* at me.

'Oh good, it is you. There's a nice article about you, good photo, too, in the Style section. Do you want it? I've finished with the paper now, so you can have the whole thing.' She handed it over.

'Thanks, love. That was the journalist who came around the week before last with that crazy photographer who wanted something different and had me outside in the rain with Carnie.'

She laughed. 'I remember. Well, you don't look cross at all in the photo, just nice.'

'I didn't feel nice.' I grinned. 'I felt like throttling him.'

Back in my flat I opened the paper, discarding the various sections, sport, finance, real estate, and finally finding my article. Carnie came to sit on the pages I'd put aside, purring and kneading her claws. I clipped the piece for my scrap-book, then noticed my flatmate being her usual destructive self.

'Don't tear it to shreds,' I admonished her, 'I want to read the rest. You can have it when I've finished.' I rescued the bulk of the paper. 'Here, have the employment section, if you must wreck something.'

The front page reported the week's doings of the Fitzgerald Inquiry in very full detail. Much speculation was being raised about certain entries in the diaries of certain ministers and a top police official, but several people had had alleged mysterious attacks of amnesia and couldn't recall what the various initials represented.

'Oh yes,' I muttered, 'and pigs might fly!'

In his evidence the officer stated he could not remember who the initials T.M. and D.W. referred to, nor why he wrote that T.M. would take care of the problem. He did recall that the other initial referred to the minister in question, but could not recall, when cross-examined, why he would have spoken with the minister, or the content of their conversation.

'Very likely,' I told Carnie sceptically. She looked up from the Situations Vacant. The phone rang and I consigned the rest of the paper to my automatic shredder, who purred with pleasure.

'Micky? Charlotte,' she said. 'I was lucky. I rang the after hours number of the domestic agency. Debbie worked for them for a few years after she left us, then went into business with a friend. Luckily, the woman I got was the lady in charge. She kept in touch with Debbie because she liked her. I pretended I wanted domestic help and she said she didn't think Debbie would be interested because she and her friend run a recycled clothing shop called Double Take—in Paddington, of all places!'

'That's great, Charlotte. Thanks for going to all that trouble.'

'Micky,' she said in a small voice, 'I hate all this, but I think you might be right. I'll back you and help you. I want to know the truth about Dad and Billy. If anyone did kill them, I want whoever it was caught and punished.'

'I'll find out what I can,' I promised, 'and I'll keep in touch, Charlotte.'

I'd put the book she'd sold me on the desk and, as Carnie wasn't about to give up the paper, I opened it and started to read. Just about everything that grows in Australia seemed to be poisonous, imports as well as home grown. I read on, fascinated. Half an hour later I was on the phone to David Reeves, tracking him down at home this time.

'Mary says don't you dare disturb my Sunday,' he cautioned. 'We've got our daughter Clara and the kids coming for afternoon tea. It's Sharon's birthday.' His granddaughter.

'I'm sorry, David,' I told him, 'but I think you need to know this.' I explained and he gave a long whistle.

'Are you serious? Yes, of course you are. Sorry! No, of course they wouldn't have checked for—I don't even know if it'd show in the bloodstream. What effect did you say? Disorientation? Hallucination? *How* deadly? My God!'

'And we know who has it, and whose special interest that is,' I commented.

'It's possible.' He hesitated. 'Look, I'll get the lab boys on to it. If you're right it would mean an exhumation, and that's not to be suggested lightly. Leave it with me, Micky, and for God's sake, don't go accusing anyone. It could be the last thing you ever do.'

CHAPTER 21

I'd no sooner replaced the receiver when the phone rang again. I must be personally responsible for most of Telecom's mind-boggling profits! Jimmy Crane's deep voice said, 'G'day, mate.'

'Jimmy! What's the news?'

'They've gone out for the arvo,' he said. 'They're not due back until dinner-time. If you want to check out the house, you'd better get up here now.'

'How do you know?' I asked, surprised. 'Do you work on a Sunday?'

He chuckled. 'No, but I know what's going on, no sweat. I'll let you in, mate.'

I parked the car discreetly out of sight, just in case, and walked the wet yards to the house. No sign of the rain letting up and an ever-increasing number of suburban streets, flooded by swollen creeks and banked-up storm-water drains, were now blocked off with barricades and warning lamps. The Council's stock of detour signs must be running low. Luckily, this area was too high and hilly to be affected.

Praying that Jimmy was right, an excuse on my lips if he wasn't, I trod down the rose-lined drive and on to the red cedar verandah, and pulled the bell. As if it was a pre-arranged signal, Su-Lin slid from shelter under the verandah, leaped up the steps with her incomparable grace, and yowled noisily, rubbing her head against my legs. Carnie would love that!

The door opened and Jimmy was grinning at me. 'Come in, mate. Hey, Su-Lin's taken to you, all right.'

'Probably smells my Abyssinian,' I said, bending to stroke the plush cream Siamese, who followed me into the hall. I put my umbrella in the stand, noticing the stockman's coat

and hat hanging on the pegs, and went with Jimmy into the
drawing-room. The front door was visible from some areas
of the elegant room, so I assumed Charlotte had been correct
when she'd remembered Sir Martin and her mother coming
in that way. Opposite, across the passageway, was another
door I'd noticed on my previous visit.

'What's through there?' I asked.

'Ballroom. It's never used now. You want to see it?'

'Oh yes.' The door opened into another high-ceilinged
room, equal in space to the full drawing-room, which now
had the carved red cedar door unfolded across the width,
halving its size. The ballroom was superb. Polished floor,
curtained alcoves, chairs and sofas all of the period, set at
intervals down the long wall; tall mirrors, which must have
reflected the dazzling lights and beautiful ball dresses of the
colonial ladies; French windows looking on to the front and
side verandahs, as in the drawing-room opposite.

'Who keeps all this clean?' I asked, awed by the beauty
of the long room with its patterned ceiling and great paintings of early Australian scenes.

'A couple of women come in twice a week. Mrs F, she's
rich. She can afford it.'

I turned to go, reluctantly. 'My aunt, my great-aunt, used
to come to balls here,' I said. 'It's fascinating. But we'd
better get on. I want to see where Trent's room was, and
Mrs Forrest's study. I didn't see all the rooms when I came
before.'

Jimmy closed the ballroom door behind us. 'No sweat.'
He led the way down the passage which branched left
around the dining-room with its family portraits and
through to William's study and Amelia's workroom.

'I've seen them.' I repressed a shudder at the thought of
William's room and noticed Jimmy watching me strangely.
'Rabbit ran over my grave,' I joked.'

'Mrs F, her bedroom's right here, next to William's
study. He pointed to the door. I didn't open it—I felt

uncomfortably like an intruder and was wishing I hadn't started this. 'Clifford, he slept next door. No one's used his room since. You can go in.' He opened the door into a large bedroom with a four-poster bed, dresser, wardrobes and chairs. The tall windows led on to the verandah and I went over. Outside, the travellers' palms were being thrashed about in a rain squall. Mrs Forrest would have the same view from her bedroom. The room was impersonal, after sixteen years of no occupation.

'Mrs F, she sleeps in William and Amelia's room,' Jimmy said. 'Her study's in the other wing.'

'May I see her study?'

'Why not, mate?' He led me back past the dining-room to where the passage branched. Mrs Forrest's study was in the same position as William's, but on the opposite side of the house.

'What's in there?' I pointed to the door opposite the dining-room.

'Billiards-room, games-room,' Jimmy said. We glanced in, then continued to Mrs Forrest's study. Feeling thoroughly embarrassed now, I pushed open her door.

The room was beautifully furnished and was dominated by an intricately carved wooden Chinese screen. Hinged into three sections, it shielded the desk from the door. Jimmy sat deliberately at the desk, as if claiming his own. Hidden by the screen, I slipped out of the room for a moment to check if the coast was still clear. I had a guilty dread of the ladies coming home early and catching us red-handed. Jimmy kept talking, unaware that I'd ducked out.

'Mrs Hill,' he was saying, 'she sleeps in this wing, at the end of the passage.'

I came back into the room. 'What?' I was surprised. 'Show me.'

Margaret's room was the fourth room along. Well, I thought, she certainly didn't hear Mrs Forrest go to bed if she was in her room, as she says. She must have been snooping around.

'All these rooms, there were bedrooms, guest-rooms. Not used now. In the old days, family, they slept on the other side. Mrs F, Mr T, Bill, and Charlotte and Amelia together until they got too big and Amelia, she moved into this wing, next to Mrs H. Except it wasn't Mrs H then. Cook slept here. Kitchen's in the middle, between both wings, so you can get to it from either side.'

'What happened to the cook?'

'Oh, she was old. Retired when they didn't need her any more. Went to live with her daughter, down south. Then Mrs H, she took over the cooking.' He stirred. 'You seen everything you want?'

'In the house, yes. Can we go outside?'

'Sure.'

I felt safer in the grounds. I collected my umbrella, Jimmy his coat and Akubra, and we turned right and went around the side. I looked at the windows, counting them. Drawing-room, dining-room, William's study, Mrs Forrest's bed-room, Clifford Trent's bedroom. All easily accessible from the side garden. A flight of steps led up to the verandah.

'I want to see the site of the well.'

'Then you go by yourself, mate.' Jimmy pointed the way and sat at his ease, oblivious of the rain, on a garden bench. 'I'll wait here.'

I found the site of the old well easily, beyond the olean-ders. A shallow depression in the ground where the well had been filled in. Here I was quite close to the fence and the overgrown hedge that stood thickly at the head of the drop which fell to the extraordinary cave below. I thought about William standing here talking to himself, if that was true, by the well which so many years before had been a spring of life-giving water that he'd deliberately turned into a death-trap. You bastard, I thought savagely, and immediately my anger seemed to flare from nothing, leaving me sick and shaken. My God, if Al Wang was right about impressions being left in a place, this place was full of hate and fear, and it was catching. No wonder Jimmy had opted to stay away from here.

Suddenly there was a jarring cry which made me jump, and Su-Lin was by me, looking fixedly at the well depression, her tail fluffed. I broke out of the vast anger that had laid hold of me and, in a sudden movement, picked her up. She went rigid with the shock of this indignity.

'Come on, Su-Lin,' I told her firmly. 'Whatever it is, we don't want to know.'

She shrugged crossly out of my arms, but had lost interest in the well and now picked her way daintily through the grass, leading me away from danger.

Jimmy was lazing on his bench, rain splashing on the brim of his hat, filling a pipe from a small, ancient leather pouch. He grinned and took care lighting the tobacco, moving the match slowly back and forth over the bowl. The familiar, sweet scent drifted in the rain which dripped wearily through the trees.

'You seen all you want at the well?' He grinned, and I'd swear he was looking into my inner thoughts, aware of my experience there.

I watched him in silence as the smoke curled up. So that's it, I thought, and sighed as another piece of the puzzle slid quietly into place. Jimmy was looking at me, the grin fading from his face. 'William walk on your grave, or was it another bloody rabbit? I told you, you're safe here as long as you keep the law. Don't get bothered, mate.'

I made up my mind. 'Jimmy, you've been great. Thanks, mate!' I held out my hand and he took it in a firm grip, but looked puzzled. 'I've got to go, and you'd better, too—to wherever you take yourself.

'You be back, mate?'

'That depends. I'll see it through, don't worry, but I have to think which is the best way. How can I contact you?'

His face shadowed. 'You can't. I'll be in touch when you need me, though. I'll know when.'

I expect you will, you cunning bastard, I said silently, then suddenly remembered. 'You said you had something to show me, when you saw me again.'

His face had changed as if he'd sensed my sudden knowing, and he looked wary, not sure what I was going to do about it.

'Yeah, well, it'll keep till later, no sweat, mate.'

CHAPTER 22

I pulled up at a phone-booth and made a dash through the rain to check the white pages. A number of Paddington shops are open on a Sunday; the small, privately owned ones, anyway. I noted the address of Double Take, crossed my fingers and followed Given Terrace down, pulling up outside the small cottage with its roofed verandah, bright paintwork and, thankfully, open front door. The verandah was hard up against the footpath, and level with it, the railings doubling as a fence. I went inside, leaving my umbrella open on the verandah to dry off.

'Hello! Can I help you?'

The woman was in her early thirties, not much more than five feet tall, trim and petite. She balanced easily on four-inch heels, which brought her up to my chest, and was wearing fashionable stone-washed jeans and a bright floral blouse. She had to be 'little Debbie'. I thought how apt the name was.

'Debbie Harris?' I asked confidently.

'Yes, you must be Micky. Micky Douglas.'

'Don't tell me you're clairvoyant!'

'No, just forewarned. Charlotte Dysart telephoned and said you wanted to talk to me.'

I was pleased, and silently thanked Charlotte for her foresight. 'Did she tell you why?'

Debbie gave me a friendly smile. 'No, but she asked me to tell you anything you want to know. I gather you're a journalist and it's for a story of some kind.'

Clever Charlotte, I thought. 'Is there somewhere we can talk?'

'Oh, sure, there are a couple of chairs at the back of the

shop. We're not likely to be disturbed. This rain's rather good at putting customers off.'

'Where's your partner?' I wondered if there were curious ears listening in the back room.

'She's not here. We do alternate weekends. There's only me.'

I followed her through the racks of clothes and she pulled a chair forward. We sat and eyed each other, me unsure of what to say, her with that friendly smile, waiting.

'Look, I know it sounds odd, but Charlotte said you might be able to tell me everything that happened at Darkwater the day William Trent died.'

Her face showed her surprise. It must have been the last thing she was expecting.

'Good heavens!' She hesitated. 'Well, yes, I can certainly do that.' She thought back. 'How much do you want to know?'

'Everything, in the order that it happened. You see, I've heard several second-hand accounts, but you were an eye-witness, weren't you?'

'Uh-huh! Well, Mr Trent had been appointed to head a Commission into the Government and William was trying to get him not to do it.'

'You knew about that?'

'Everyone in the house knew about it. They'd shouted at each other for an hour in the drawing-room, the day before. No one could fail to hear *something*. Mrs Forrest-Trent had tried to stop them, but then something happened. I had the impression that Mr Trent had backed down.'

'What?'

'Oh, William could get him to do anything, in the end. It often happened. They'd yell and argue—Mr Trent wasn't very—' she searched for a word—'he was a bit weak, if you know what I mean, and he'd rage and shout to hide it and to get in first. I reckon he knew if he listened to William he'd always get talked round.'

'And you think it happened in this case?'

'I'm sure of it. Because the next day I was doing the cleaning in the hall, by the billiards-room, next to Mrs Forrest-Trent's study. Mr Trent went in to see her and didn't close the door. I don't expect he noticed me—I was just around the corner. Anyway, he said he'd agreed with William and he was going to give it up and tell the truth. She sounded very sharp and said he couldn't, and he said, "If I don't, William will."' Debbie paused and shrugged slightly. 'I'm only human, so I listened at the door. We were all mad to know what was going on. Then Mrs Forrest-Trent said she'd talk to William and it was important for the family that he didn't proceed. She said he was a Forrest and he'd see reason.' Debbie laughed. 'William was really only half a Forrest, but he was heir to Darkwater and all Forrest in his mother's eyes. I suppose she thought it would be good for the family if Mr Trent headed the Commission. They said he'd get a knighthood if he did. She'd have been Lady Forrest-Trent.'

'What happened then?'

'Well, that was the end of it, until William arrived, all bright and sunny and confident that his father agreed with him. He brought some papers. Mrs Forrest-Trent came out of her study and said, "Come in here, William," and he went into her room.' Debbie's eyes twinkled. 'You can bet I hung around, but the door was closed. I went into the billiards-room and pretended to clean, but all I could hear was a mumble of voices. I was *so* curious.' She laughed unashamedly. 'Then they started fighting and I heard a word here and there. William shouted about signing and that would confirm it; at least, I think that's what he said, and his mother said something about the family and she'd stop him, but I don't know if she meant William or Mr Trent. Then William went out of her room and slammed the door fit to break it, and I hurried out to see him storming off to his father's room.' She stopped suddenly. 'Is this what you want?'

'Yes, yes, perfect,' I said anxiously. 'Go on.'

'I heard William shout, "Is this true?" as he went into his father's study, then Mrs Forrest-Trent came out and saw me and told me to go and get Margaret Hill.'

I frowned. 'Margaret was in the house?'

'Oh yes, she'd come by earlier to pick up a recipe she'd left with Cook the day before. I went and got her and she took herself off. I stayed in the kitchen then. I didn't want to get caught. Mrs Forrest-Trent was in a bad enough temper.'

'So you didn't see what happened next?'

'Yes I did. Mrs Hill was gone about ten minutes and when she came back she said Mrs Forrest-Trent wanted a cuppa and she'd got William to have a cup and talk rationally about it all. Mrs Hill made the coffee and poured two cups, one for William and his mother's special one, and took the tray out. Then she came back, but she went home after I'd told them what had happened.'

'What did you do then?'

'I went back, seeing as how everything had calmed down. I thought Mr Trent might like a cuppa as well, but all he wanted was a brandy. He looked ghastly. I saw the papers William brought on his desk, but I couldn't get a good look. Anyway, as I went out, I heard him say to himself, "You know, the boy's right. It has to stop."'

'So it was his mother William rowed with before he stormed off?'

'Oh no, they were quite calm. About twenty minutes later they walked to the front door together, arm in arm. Mrs Forrest-Trent said, "You can't stop him. Think of the family." William said, "I am thinking of it and I won't give in." Then she said, "I'm sorry, William, but I'll have to stop you."'

I leaned forward excitedly. 'What did he say?'

'He just laughed. He kissed her on the cheek and said, "You can't Mum, I won't let you." Then he put on his raincoat—it'd been teeming—and went off. I heard that sports car of his revving up and driving away.'

'How come you remember it all so clearly?' I asked her. 'It was sixteen years ago.'

'Ah. I remember everything about William Trent. He was a real good-looker. Could charm the birds out of the trees, that one. I had a real crush on him and I sort of watched him, you see.'

'Margaret said he left in a temper after a row with his father, and stormed out of the house. She said you told her.'

She shrugged again. 'That silly old bat! She wouldn't know if she was Arthur or Martha, or what day it was. She's got muddled up.'

'She also said she wasn't there.'

'Oh yes? She probably mixed her days up. She was always there, the old cow. Pretending to be so sorry when I got the sack. Did you know about that? A vase got smashed in the drawing-room and Mrs Forrest-Trent said I did it, then Mrs Hill went all holy and said I was a bad girl to lie and she'd never have believed it of me, the old fraud.' She was indignant. 'I never broke the damned thing, but Cook said Mrs Hill had been in the room and she must have done it. But she'd never have admitted it, so I got the sack.'

'I'm sorry,' I said, not knowing what else to say.

'Oh, goodness, I'm not. I did pretty well after I left there and now I've got my own little shop. I'm all right. I just get mad about the vase, 'cause I knew it wasn't me.'

I grinned at her, liking her and her bright smile and the way she freely admitted to eavesdropping, not trying to pretend she wasn't curious.

'Did you ever tell your story to the police?'

'Well, now, I was never asked. After all, William's death was an accident. Funny—' she frowned—'you know, I hadn't thought about it for a long time but I thought he'd been drinking. Then they said no alcohol in his blood, so I was wrong.'

'What made you think that?'

'I'm not sure. It was just an impression. Hang on a minute.' Her brow creased and she looked back into time. 'Oh yes, I remember. He stumbled slightly in the hall when he was putting his mac on. And he sounded a bit distant. It was just the faintest impression, as I said, and I was obviously wrong.'

I'll bet you weren't, I thought.

'You know, Mrs Hill probably said she wasn't there because Mrs Forrest-Trent told her not to talk about it. She would, you know, she'd hush it up that the family had problems. Always had to show a united front, the Trents. And as for saying that William stormed out, well, she always did exaggerate a lot. Made things dramatic. In her mind she probably really believes that. I was pretty upset when he died. I thought he was wonderful, not that he looked at me, but it didn't stop me thinking he was fabulous. Well, I was sixteen, he was twenty-five, and such a—what do they say these days? A spunk? That was William. It was just bad luck. He drove the MG like he was at Le Mans most of the time.' She stopped as a woman peered tentatively through the door.

'Come in, we're open.'

The woman looked startled. 'Oh no, thanks, just looking,' and she hurried off in the rain which had begun to roar on the iron roof.

'Oh well,' Debbie sighed. 'It will get better when this wretched weather clears up.' Her voice was raised against the noise. 'We do pretty well, usually. Is there anything more I can tell you?'

I got up. 'No, you've been a tremendous help.' I put out my hand and she shook it warmly.

'Any time. We've got men's gear, too. Come again and browse.'

'You're on,' I promised. 'See you later.'

She accompanied me to the door. 'Don't get drowned out there.'

The downpour was overflowing the gutter and cascading off the verandah roof. I waved and plunged out into the wet.

That night the rain bucketed down, the wind whipping around my flat, forcing its way under the windows in a howling, lashing fury. I tried to shut out the threatening sound of it, going over and over the past week in my mind, then on paper; times, dates, people, putting it all together, needing to know for my own peace of mind. Finally, well after midnight, I thought I had it. It was logical, it fitted.

'I know; bloody hell, I know!' I exulted. 'Why William was killed, why Clifford, and then poor bloody Bob. All for what? For the bloody family! But how the hell do I prove it? David? David couldn't have been party to a cover-up. But then, look at the Fitzgerald Inquiry. Is it safe to trust anyone? What will happen to me if I tell David? Or will the evidence, if there is any, just quietly disappear? Oh hell, what do I do?'

Hours later I got to bed, but I slept badly, the thunder shaking the sky to pieces and sending down more solid rain and rain and rain and . . .

The dawn arrived in complete silence, except for the water riveting from all points of the roof, every tree-trunk a waterfall draining from the heavy, rain-laden leaves; the sky grey and still, but mercifully intact. I went down in my pyjamas and put Carnie out, then came back to my typewriter. Inserting a fresh sheet of paper I began typing furiously, my fingers flying, my head finally clear.

By seven, I'd called a taxi, dressed, and was waiting on the footpath. The car pulled up next to me and I gave the driver the envelope and paid the fee.

'Make sure they know it's to be given to Inspector David Reeves personally, no one else, as soon as he arrives. It's most urgent.'

The driver gave me a jaundiced look and fingered the

envelope. 'That what it says here? Inspector David Reeves, Urgent, Private and Confidential?'

'Yes, yes, that's right.'

'Yeah, well, I think I can handle that,' he said witheringly, and drove off.

I grinned and went back upstairs. Always start the day with a good breakfast, my mother had told us. It puts a lining on your stomach and gives you energy. Well, I needed energy now, to face the unknown day and all the fear that was welling up in me. I looked at the calendar in disbelief. It was only a week ago that Bob, armed with whatever knowledge he had, had rung Mrs Forrest and had been invited to Darkwater. Only last Monday! And here was a new Monday to be dealt with.

Carnie came to sit by my chair, in case there were any scraps to be had. 'You'd better go to Monica today,' I told her, rubbing her beautiful red-gold head. 'I'll take you down later. You see, love, I've got something to do and—and I may not be back until late. And if I didn't happen to come home at all, well, Monica would look after you.'

She looked up at me with her frank green eyes, hearing the disquiet in my voice, and followed me to the phone.

'Micky,' Al had told me, many times. 'Always trust your feelings. Your logical conclusions aren't always the most reliable, but I've never seen you go wrong when you go with your gut. It's a real gift, my friend. You should always listen inside.'

I wish I'd listened to him. It might have changed the outcome, who knows? I'm sometimes very thick.

I picked up the receiver and dialled.

CHAPTER 23

Once again I parked in the narrow side lane against the Darkwater fence. The tall bamboo stems were quiet in the dead calm of the day. Water still dripped from trees and bushes and drained down the gutters. The air was noticeably cooler, with the dry touch of approaching winter on its breath.

As I pushed open the tall, wrought-iron gates there was a loud cry and Su-Lin, from her vantage-point on the gate-post, greeted me affectionately and came down the palm tree to wind herself around my legs, mewing in her distinctive way.

I walked with her down the driveway. The roses had taken a battering and the last of the summer petals littered the ground. I noticed Jimmy Crane in the distance, repairing the storm-damaged greenery by the fence and he started towards me, then changed his mind, but continued to stare as I went up the steps. The shutters were open, and all the windows, airing the house. Once again, Margaret answered my ring, looking suspicious. She was wearing an enveloping apron with a large front pocket.

'What did you say to her?' she whispered. 'She's quite disturbed.'

'Nothing,' I said casually. 'Just that I had something to say which concerned her. Has she been in the garden?'

Margaret stopped and stared. 'How did you know? Yes, poor Eileen, and she looks quite worn out.'

'I'll try not to make it worse,' I promised, and she took me down the right-hand passage to Mrs Forrest's study. The house was cold and bleak, like everything else today. She tapped on the door and opened it.

'He's here, dear.'

'Come in, Mr Douglas.'

I went around the carved Chinese screen. Mrs Forrest was sitting at her desk, upright and regal, outwardly smiling but her eyes wary. There was a fire crackling cheerfully in the fireplace, warming and drying the room. Margaret went out, leaving us together.

'Thank you for seeing me, Mrs Forrest.'

She waved me to a chair. 'I was intrigued. Something that concerned me—and my deceased husband and son? Yes, I am most interested to hear what you have to say. Perhaps you will begin.'

You know how she does it, my inner voice whispered, against the hammering of my heart. You're pre-warned and therefore safe. She hasn't the physical strength to do it any other way, unless she's got a gun in the drawer. Be careful, watch her every move. I schooled my face to be as calm as she was.

'It began with Bob Slater,' I said carefully. 'During his research on the Darkwater article, he found something that worried him—something that made him think your son had been deliberately killed.'

She sat even straighter, but said nothing.

'I assume none of this is new to you, because I believe that Bob came to see you last Monday and told you his suspicions, and that he was killed before he could go any further.'

She gave me an icy smile. 'You are not, of course, suggesting that I had anything to do with the death of your friend?'

It obviously wasn't beat around the bush time. She was way ahead of me.

'I think you could have, and I think you had a motive. What I want to know is, did you?'

She shook her head slowly. 'Oh no, Mr Douglas, you could hardly expect me to admit to such a monstrous suggestion. Suppose you tell me everything you . . . think you know, and we'll see.'

I drew a deep breath. 'I think I'd better tell you that, before I came here, I detailed everything I suspect and what led me to my conclusions and sent the information to Inspector David Reeves of Homicide. He'll have it now and, if anything should happen to me he'll know why.'

To my surprise, she gave me an approving nod. 'That was wise,' she said. 'You should always have contingency plans before taking what may be called—dangerous action. By the way, your great-aunt, Melanie, rang me yesterday. I had no idea you were related to my old friend. She told me you were a very sensible young man and now I see she was quite right. Now, why do you think I killed Mr Slater?'

I had a suspicion that she was laughing at me and my gut twisted. Something's wrong, my inner voice said. You've known it since yesterday. I ignored it and began my story.

'Bob was originally a crime reporter,' I said, 'and he was very, very good. He had a nose for anything that was the least bit fishy. He left a note, "How did William really die?" I found out that many Williams had died here but, after investigating them as well as I could, I came to the conclusion that the William was your son, William Trent.'

She made no sign, just listened, her head bent slightly towards me. I went on.

'I'd been told by several people that your husband and son had been fighting about his appointment to the Commission into Government corruption. The general belief was that William didn't want him to take the job because he thought it would just be another cover-up, a whitewash, but that Mr Trent thought he could do some good. Also, that it might mean a knighthood. You tried to stop your son from influencing his father because you wanted him to take the job. But I don't believe that any more.'

She stirred. 'What do you think was the truth?' she asked, still cool, still courteous.

I took a breath. Now for the biggie. 'I saw yesterday's paper in which the initials T.M. and D.W. were mentioned in the police commissioner's diary, and that he conveniently didn't recall what they meant. But I believe T.M. was your husband.'

'My husband's initials were C.T.,' she said nicely, 'but do go on.'

'I will,' I said grimly. 'John Curtis told me your husband's colleagues called him The Mountie. T.M., you see, and the D.W. had to be Darkwater. I've heard how honest and straightforward your son was. I believe your husband, who I was told was a weak man and easily manipulated, was one of the top legal people who was a party to the corruption and knew very well the Commission was to be a white-wash—he'd be able to make sure of that, being in charge. And for his reward, a knighthood was offered. I believe William found out what was going on and tried to get his father to break with his colleagues' influence and tell the truth, and that he'd agreed to that in the end. But you knew it would be a terrible blow to the family if it came out he'd been part of all that corruption, and you tried to stop William. When you realized you couldn't you killed him to stop him talking, because he'd threatened, hadn't he, that he'd tell the truth if his father didn't.'

She flinched slightly, but gave no other sign. 'You think I could have killed my only son?'

'I think it's possible, if it came to a choice between an individual and the honour of the family and Darkwater.'

Her face was pale. 'Perhaps, yes, I don't know. How am I supposed to have done this murder?'

'You had coffee with him before he left and as he went out your maid said she thought he was drunk. He stumbled and his speech wasn't normal. She noticed, because she had a crush on him so was watching him very closely. I think you put something into his drink and it had just begun to take effect. You'd been in the garden, pruning oleanders. Oleander is a deadly hallucinogenic; but you'd know that, with your background in botany, and any bitterness would be well disguised in the unusually strong flavour of the Darkwater coffee.'

'I see.' She frowned faintly. 'Then what was I supposed to have done?'

I could see that, behind her eyes, her mind was otherwise engaged.

'I think you spread the story about William going off in a rage, and deliberately sacked the only person who might refute the story. Debbie Harris didn't break that vase, you know. I wonder if you did it yourself? Anyway, now your family was safe, until the funeral.'

'What about the funeral?' Her voice was hard now, and icy.

'Your husband must have felt himself responsible for his son's death, believing William had gone straight from a row with him to his death. I was told he looked ghastly at the funeral gathering and went to lie down, but then asked everyone to wait as he had something to tell them. You must have realized he was going to confess the whole thing. He probably told you he would. I believe he wanted to. So you took the gun from William's study, went out into the side garden, up the steps to the verandah, through the French windows into Mr Trent's room and shot him, making it look like suicide, then ran back out through the garden and in through the front door. You could have done it easily. You've probably always hung your garden coat and gloves in the hall. You could have slipped the gloves on as you went out and put them back in the coat pocket as you came back in, making sure there were no other fingerprints but your husband's.'

'And then I killed your friend because he knew too much?' she asked quietly.

'The same way you killed William. You took Bob into your study, Margaret brought the coffee and you sent her away. You'd been in the garden again earlier. You probably suspected what Bob knew, or he told you, and you decided to shut him up, so you gathered more oleander, made your poison, and put it in Bob's coffee. It took about the same time as with William to take effect and, as they took the same road, they came to grief in the same place. Only there was an eyewitness to Bob's accident.' Her head came up and she looked at me, eyes steady. 'Yes,' I told her, 'a man who said Bob was drunk, veering all over the road. Probably hallucinating out of his mind and just about dead, poor Bob. But there wasn't any excess of alcohol in his bloodstream, just like William.'

'I see.' She looked down at her hands, clasped on the desk. 'That really is an ingenious theory.'

'It's the only way it could have been. It all ties in, it fits all the facts. You're quite fanatical about Darkwater and I think you'd do just about anything to save it from disgrace.'

She looked up and said levelly, 'Ah, but now you're here, and what am I to do about you, Mr Douglas?'

I forced my voice not to shake. 'Nothing, if you're wise. David Reeves knows everything.'

'But you'd like me to confess, to admit that you are right.'

'What other explanation is there?'

She sighed. 'What indeed? As you say, it all ties in, it fits the facts, the only thing is—' she gave me a brief smile—'I didn't do it, Mr Douglas. You may think I could kill my husband and child for a history and a name, and I suppose I must have given you that impression. If so, I'm sorry. I think I would give my life to keep Darkwater safe, if that was required of me, but I would gladly sacrifice Darkwater and all my family history to have my beloved William back. You can believe that or not, it really doesn't matter. If I am guilty of anything, it is that I didn't voice my dreadful suspicions earlier. Perhaps I was, in a way, responsible for Mr Slater's death but never William, never Clifford. You see, I didn't know—then. Your friend's death has shaken me badly. It has reminded me of all that tragedy, and what I chose to overlook.'

I stared at her, feeling numb. Something was terribly wrong with my brilliant theory. I'd sensed it and, like a complete moron, I'd gone rushing off with a stupid, logical plan which was perfect, but wrong. If anyone was telling the truth it was Eileen Forrest. No one was that good an actress.

'What suspicions?' I asked, my confidence in tatters; but before I could go on she held up an imperious hand as a slight noise came from the door.

'Is that you, Margaret?' she called. 'Come in, dear.'

CHAPTER 24

Margaret Hill's face appeared anxiously around the screen.

'I thought you'd like something,' she said, 'so I made coffee. Are you all right, Eileen?' She looked closely at her friend and frowned in my direction. 'Micky hasn't been saying anything to *upset* you, has he, dear?'

'I'm perfectly all right. Would you like to join us, Margaret?'

'No, no, dear. I'll just see you have everything, then I'll go.' She handed Mrs Forrest the delicate Chinese cup. The aroma of good strong Darkwater coffee filled the room. 'I hope I've remembered the way you like yours, Micky. Now, a biscuit? You liked my shortbread, didn't you?'

'Yes, delicious.' I took a piece. Mrs Forrest was drinking, her eyes on me. I lifted my cup.

'I wouldn't drink it, Mr Douglas.' Mrs Forrest's voice was calm. She put down her cup and reached over, quietly taking mine away. 'It wouldn't be very wise, would it, Margaret?'

Margaret Hill's eyes swivelled from her friend to me, and back to Mrs Forrest. She gave a little laugh.

'Why, Eileen, dear, whatever are you talking about?'

'I promised Mr Douglas's aunt that no harm would come to him. You remember Melanie Carter-Jones? Mr Douglas is her great-nephew. And he's a friend of Su-Lin, dear. You wouldn't want to hurt him.'

'But, Eileen, what are you saying? Let him drink his coffee, dear. It'll go cold.'

'Perhaps I'd better drink it.' She lifted my cup to her lips and Margaret screamed.

'No, no, Eileen, put it down!' She reached out in a panic and pulled the cup away, splashing the desktop and carpet.

'Margaret!' Mrs Forrest's voice was stern. 'What have you done?'

'N-nothing, really, Eileen: what has Micky said about me? He doesn't think it was me, he thinks it was you!'

'Have you been listening at the door, again?'

'Oh no, no, Eileen, I only heard a little.'

'And that was enough.' Mrs Forrest stood up, reaching for her cane, leaning on it heavily. She looked suddenly exhausted.

'Margaret, I know all about it. God help me, I think I always knew but couldn't bring myself to believe it.' She turned to me. 'Your theory does fit, Mr Douglas, but it was Margaret, not me.'

'I don't believe it!' I was aghast.

'Then finish your coffee, Mr Douglas. What did you use, Margaret? Was it oleander? Like William and Mr Slater?' Her voice was suddenly like a whiplash, and Margaret cringed. 'Did you kill my son?'

'He didn't mind, really,' Margaret whispered. 'I told him, it was for the family. I had to. And for you, dear. If I hadn't, he'd have dragged down poor Clifford and you and all of us. But he didn't mind; he came back, so he couldn't have minded.'

I stared at her. 'What do you mean—came back?' I demanded.

'Oh, he did, Micky, *really* he did. He goes down into the servants' rooms and smokes, just the way he used to, the naughty boy. I tell him often that you won't have his pipe in the house, Eileen, but he still does it.'

'Margaret.' Mrs Forrest was suddenly gentle. 'Tell me everything, my dear. No one will hurt you, I promise. Just tell me the truth.'

Tears were flooding down Margaret's face. 'I thought you'd *want* me to do it, to save the Family,' she wailed. 'Eileen, you *know* William was going to hurt us all. You said you wished you could stop him. I remembered you once told me how to make a rat poison from oleander, and I still had some, so I thought: I'll stop him for you. I'd do anything for you, Eileen, anything. You know that, dear.'

'Yes, I know.' Eileen Forrest sat down again, unable to stand any longer. She looked a broken woman. 'And Clifford? Was that you, too?'

'You won't be angry?' Margaret's faded blue eyes were awash with tears.

'I promise. Just tell the truth.'

'Well, I knew how to use the gun, of course. You showed us that Christmas. I'd gone to make a cup of tea for everyone, after the funeral. I'd heard Clifford tell you he couldn't go on, he was going to confess and face his punishment. Then he told everyone to wait and I knew I had to stop him quickly. I got the gun from William's study. I knew *he* wouldn't mind if I used it, not to save Darkwater. I went to Clifford's room. He was asleep. It was very easy. I knew to use gloves and I had a pair in my handbag from the funeral, so I'd got them out and I slipped them back when I came in. No one noticed.'

Eileen Forrest bowed her head. 'I noticed,' she said slowly, 'but it never occurred to me that you had—I thought you'd just left them somewhere and were returning them to your bag.' She faced her friend. 'So when Mr Slater came to see me last Monday, you must have listened at the door and heard him tell me he suspected William had been murdered, and Clifford.'

Margaret blanched. She was shaking and weeping softly. 'I wanted to know about the article. I thought he might read it, and then I could hear what he'd written. But he said he was sure William and Clifford had been murdered and he would have to go to the police. So I asked William.' A cunning look came into her eyes and she nodded wisely. 'I asked William, and he said, "Use the poison you used on me," so I did. It was easy. You always use *your* cup, so I knew you were in no danger. I'd never hurt *you*, Eileen, never. Or the Family. I *love* Darkwater. I'll *always* keep it safe.'

'I know, dear, I know.' Mrs Forrest looked sad. 'If I hadn't tried to instill in you a sense of pride, told you about our history, made it important to you—I feel I'm to blame. You're not—you're not—responsible, dear. I've known that for a long time, now. William's curse is still as strong as it ever was.'

Margaret looked at me suddenly, and there was a menace in her eyes. I flinched and felt my scalp crawl.

'But now there's *him*,' she said quietly. 'Now he knows, dear. What will I do?'

'Nothing, Margaret, he won't drink the coffee. I promised Melanie to keep him safe, so I must.'

'But you can't!' Margaret's voice rose sharply. 'He'll *tell*, Eileen. If he won't drink the coffee, then I'll use this.'

She reached into her wide pocket and brought out an old-fashioned hand gun, levelling it at me. Eileen Forrest gasped and got to her feet, moving slowly towards her friend.

'No, Margaret, that's not a good idea. Give me the gun.'

'I can't,' Margaret said reasonably. 'You can see that, Eileen. I have to stop him, for the Family. Don't you care about the Family any more?'

'Yes, dear, but this is wrong.' She was making her way cautiously around the desk. I sat, paralysed by Margaret's insane eyes and set face. I couldn't move a muscle and my mouth was dry.

She really means it, my mind chattered in total panic.

'Margaret, give it to me.'

I saw her finger begin to tighten as Mrs Forrest, in strange slow motion, threw herself forward. Minutes later, it seemed, there was an explosion and the last mistress of Darkwater fell slowly to the floor and lay motionless in a crumpled heap.

Margaret screamed and dropped the gun. I hastily grabbed it as she flung herself on her friend.

'Eileen, no! Eileen!' Her voice rose shrilly as she screamed at me. 'You've killed her, it was you! She tried to save you and you killed her!'

'Eh?' I said. I'd managed to stand up and moved a step towards her, but she backed away.

'Don't come near me,' she shouted. 'You want to kill me, too.' Before I could stop her, she bent swiftly and pulled a burning branch from the fire. 'Don't come any closer. I'll defend myself, I'll defend Darkwater. You want to bring us all down.'

'Margaret, for God's sake!' I stepped closer and she swung the branch in my face.

'I mean it, Micky, don't move!'

I stopped, appalled, wondering how on earth to deal with the situation, when a sound which had begun faintly in the distance and was growing louder every second suddenly got my attention.

'Margaret, listen,' I said urgently. 'It's the police. Do you hear the siren? I told the police and they know everything. You'd better put that down. You don't want to be in any more trouble.'

She looked frightened. 'I'm not in any trouble. Eileen said she'd look after me, and now she's dead and you killed her. You'll be the one in trouble. I won't let you get away with it.'

She'd backed up to the window, trying to see the police car, and I realized with horror that the burning branch was touching the curtains. They began to smoulder and a bright flame ran up.

'Margaret, look out! You're setting the place on fire.'

I lunged forward and began to tear down the flaming material. Mistaking my action for an attack, she screamed and fled past me, bits of burning bark flying off as she flailed the wood around. I stamped at them. The sirens were getting closer and I ran after Margaret, praying I could stop her.

She turned at bay in the drawing-room, screaming, the dreadful sound going on and on, then, to my horror, she began to touch the fire to the curtains there. The flames ran up swiftly.

'You won't have it,' she screamed at me, her glasses askew and her face flushed and tear-stained. 'I won't let you have Darkwater. It's mine, do you hear me? Mine and William's.'

There were voices outside and someone was pounding on the front door. Margaret fled past me and ran down the passage. The door opened with a crash and Jimmy Crane leaped through.

'You OK, mate? I heard a shot, and screaming.' Then his eyes widened.

'Jimmy, get something to put out the fire,' I yelled desperately. 'Margaret's gone completely mad. She's torching the place.'

'Flaming hell!' He looked aghast, then said urgently, 'The cats, mate, where're the bloody cats?'

'Oh God!' I stared blankly. 'Su-Lin came in with me—I don't know.'

'They might be downstairs. I'll go around the back.'

I clutched at him. 'Jimmy, the house. What about Darkwater?'

'Hang Darkwater!' he yelled, and took off like a rocket through the front door. 'Let it bloody burn.'

'No!' I grabbed a vase and threw the contents over the flames. 'All that history? This wonderful house? No! Damn you, Jimmy!' I grabbed a cushion and began to beat at the fire, the smoke thickening around me, choking me.

Dimly I was aware of the sirens wailing, then stopping abruptly. The ceiling was beginning to blacken but I fought on in blind, shocked fury, yelling 'No, no, no!'

Someone was holding me from behind, pinioning my arms. 'Micky, for God's sake, get out of here!'

'Let me go, David! I can't let it burn!'

'The fire brigade's on the way. Leave it, Micky, the whole place is alight.'

I was sobbing in impotent fury, fighting to get free. He yelled at me in anger. Suddenly I stopped and stared around in shock. Fire was in the passageway, the drawing-room was well burning, the priceless red cedar screen a flaming barrier.

'Where's Margaret? David, Margaret Hill's in there somewhere, and Mrs Forrest—she's dead. Margaret shot her, but it was an accident. It should have been me . . .'

Through the roar of the flames a shrill, mad scream sounded, and then was abruptly cut off. David pulled the blackened cushion out of my hands and led me out. Two police cars were in the driveway, a group of men playing garden hoses on the fire. Jimmy Crane squatted nearby, holding two terrified cats. The fire engines wailed in the distance.

'Jimmy?' I felt stunned, and more exhausted than I'd have believed.

'Here, take Su-Lin.' He calmly handed over the frightened Siamese. 'She likes you.'

CHAPTER 25

It was David's idea that we gather in my flat. The police had rung Charlotte and she'd come straight up to Dark-water, which was now only a charred and blackened ruin with a couple of tall hand-made brick chimney stacks still standing, surrounded by its beautiful gardens which, merci-fully, had escaped being too damaged. A few roses and azaleas had been trampled or broken under the firemen's boots and hoses.

Jimmy and I waited for Charlotte and comforted her as best we could as she stared white-faced at where her family home had been, tears running silently down her face. For me, the scale of the tragedy was so enormous as I thought of the priceless antiques, paintings and history destroyed so completely and with such appalling speed, that I felt sick at heart, guilty and speechless.

David took me aside. 'Micky, could you get all the people concerned together? Anyone who can shed any light on this. I'd like to see Miss Bates and John Curtis, and ask Mrs Carter-Jones to join us. It might be more comfortable to meet at your place, if you don't mind. I don't think we need to drag everyone into the police station.'

Jimmy, Su-Lin and Mao came with me and Jimmy settled the confused animals in my bedroom, barricading the stairs, while I began telephoning. He was back as I finished.

'They can't get out, but seeing as they've both gone under your bed, I don't think they'll be moving for a while.' He grinned. 'What about a cuppa, mate?'

I stared at him. 'It doesn't bother you at all, does it? That fabulous old place, all that history!'

He shook his head. 'It was a dark place, that. Evil place. Yeah, it was old, and beautiful, and it's a shame, but I'm thinking there's a place much more beautiful to me, much more ancient, thousands of years old, mate, and a tradition that goes back to the Dreaming; and that place is safe, now. That house, that family, they nearly destroyed it forever. Something good, something in harmony with the land. Not just the place, but the idea of it, see?' He struggled to explain, but I got the point. 'Didn't you feel it? The curse is finished, the place at peace now, all quiet. All the evil, all the hate and fear gone in the fire. Nothing left.'

I heard my voice saying, 'So what do you do about evil?' and David Reeves's smiling reply, 'The ancients believed fire was the best antidote. The cleansing flame.'

Dear God, I thought, was it really necessary? Such a drastic cleansing? Did the evil William do strike so deep?

Joss arrived, looking somehow different—more peaceful than she'd been for days, and—lighter. I couldn't put my finger on the change. She was wrapped up in a man's leather jacket and grinned cheerfully. 'What an ending to a story!' she said excitedly.

John Curtis's voice came through the intercom and I let him in. David Reeves arrived with Charlotte and a constable who sat in a corner with a notepad on his knees, and Joss helped me serve drinks. When Laney arrived, agog to hear the story, David took charge.

'There are a lot of questions I'm sure we all want answered,' he said in his quiet, authoritative way, 'and I hope we'll clear up everything together. I believe each of us has a clue to the tragedy that happened today.' He turned to me. 'Micky, perhaps you'd like to begin. Your envelope was on my desk when I arrived at work. As soon as I read the contents I got a team together and we were on our way when we got a call on the radio that there was trouble at Darkwater. We stepped on it, but arrived too late.'

'Who told you?' I asked, and Jimmy coughed modestly.

'I did, mate. Knew you were heading for strife and I slipped in and listened at the door. Then I took off for the phone-box across the street. When I came back I heard all the commotion.'

'My God, Margaret!' All eyes went to David, who shook his head.

'I'm sorry, she didn't make it,' he said gently. 'We—we're looking for her remains, and those of Mrs Forrest now.'

Everyone fell silent and I began my story, starting with Bob and following through my growing suspicions. As succinctly as possible, I detailed my conversation with Eileen Forrest, and the dreadful realization that it had been Margaret all along.

Charlotte stared at me, horror in her eyes. 'I knew she was batty and full of the Family,' she said, 'but I'd no idea she'd do a thing like that. Why? Why? It doesn't make sense. She wasn't even a Forrest.'

Laney held up her hand. 'I think it is time for me to speak,' she said firmly. 'Micky told you that Eileen deliberately saved him because of a promise to me.'

I nodded. 'Was it because of the old favour she owed you, Laney?'

She sighed. 'Yes, dear, and she repaid it with her life. Poor Eileen. I swore I would never tell what I knew; it would have been a most dreadful scandal, but now it can't hurt her, and I feel you have a right to know. It explains a great deal.'

She had our full attention as she told her story. 'It's very simple. Eileen's father was a highly respected barrister, a pillar of society, but he had a weakness for women. His mistress, Beverley Blake, became pregnant.'

'Beverley *Blake*?' I gasped. '*Margaret*?'

She nodded. 'Margaret Hill was Michael Forrest's illegitimate daughter, Eileen's half-sister. A Forrest, you see. She never knew, but Eileen found out and took Margaret under her wing. She believed strongly that blood was thicker than water, and the Forrests had to help each other. She and her father kept the secret until, one day, I inadvertently heard them discussing Margaret. They were worried because she'd begun to show certain—Forrest traits. There's a recognizable—weakness that comes out in the Forrests from time to time, a mental weakness. It came from the first William, I believe. So sad. So I told Eileen what I'd heard and she swore me to secrecy and said she would one day return the favour.' She looked at me. 'I never needed to ask her, until I realized you were in danger. I didn't believe it was from her, but I believed it had something to do with Darkwater, and that she would take care of you there.'

I couldn't meet her eyes. 'Laney, I'm so sorry,' I stammered. 'If it hadn't been for me jumping to the wrong conclusion: and yet it never did feel quite right—perhaps if I'd waited, not been so quick to accuse her, she'd still be alive.'

'And you might be dead!' she said sharply. 'Stop feeling sorry for yourself, my boy. What's done is done, you can't go back. Margaret had obviously gone over the edge years ago, and Eileen kept her with her in spite of her suspicions, thinking no doubt that she could control her.'

'Micky, please,' Charlotte said shakily, 'I didn't know she was my aunt, and I'm feeling pretty awful right now, remembering some of the things we said about her, when she was family all along. Perhaps, if she'd known that, and knew she really did belong—she was so proud that she had a family name—perhaps she might have been different. But that wasn't our decision, and Mrs Carter-Jones is right. William, the first William, went mad, you know. He shot himself, nobody else killed him. Christopher has his early diary—the family thought it had been lost, but Adrian had taken it when he left Darkwater, I think perhaps as a hold over his father because of how he murdered the aboriginal tribe. It's very clear he was pretty uncontrollable at times, but he was such a strong man, he fought it all his life, except at the end. He wrote to Adrian, raving about the ghosts at the well and how they'd never let him sleep. He said he'd pleaded with them and pleaded with them, but he knew he was cursed. One day, I believe, he just couldn't take it any more and ended his life. I don't believe all that rubbish about the curse. I think you carry your own curse with you. William's curse was that he was mad and ruthless and thought himself above God. And he passed that curse down through his line. That's what my mother meant when she said the curse was still working. She meant it was in Margaret's blood. And my grandfather had the same streak in him. Some, like Mother, inherited the strength, the family pride, the love of history and, yes, the ruthlessness. Some just inherited the other. Margaret was a true Forrest—why didn't we see it? The intense pride and the madness, the desire to link herself with the Family. Sooner or later, anything might have pushed her over the edge, even Mum herself. I always wondered why Mum tolerated her—now I know.'

Joss stirred. 'I wish Bob's notes hadn't disappeared. I'd have liked to know if he knew all this.'

'Ah!' Jimmy got up and went to where his coat was hanging. He drew an envelope from the pocket and handed it to me with a grin. It was addressed to him, care of a post office box number. I opened it curiously. Inside were several sheets of neat handwriting.

'Bob's notes!' Joss gasped and craned to see. I stared at Jimmy's widening grin. 'He posted them to you? Why the hell didn't you tell me?'

He shrugged. 'Sorry, mate. I was going to later, when I was sure about you. I told you I had something else to show you. He didn't get as far as you. Picked up about Clifford being involved in the corruption and him and Bill being murdered but didn't jump to it being Mrs F.' I groaned, and he looked pained. 'Well, how was I to know you were going to come charging in like a bull at a gate and accuse people?'

I rounded on him. 'You didn't help. Margaret was sure Bill Trent was still around because of the smoke in the servants' quarters.' I didn't admit I had almost come to the same conclusion. I already felt enough like an idiot. 'But it was you, wasn't it? You were squatting down there with the cats, and smoking your damned pipe.'

'Only sometimes,' he said mildly. 'Not every night. It was the only way I could stay there, keep watch. The ladies, they never knew. I thought you realized yesterday, when I was lighting up. I thought you might have decided to tell them.'

'No, they never knew,' I said, 'but it all added to Margaret's madness. I don't understand why Mrs Forrest never noticed the smell—or perhaps she thought her son was haunting the place as well.'

Charlotte was looking at us. 'Was it you, Jimmy? Margaret said something to me once, quite seriously, about Billy still smoking downstairs. I thought she was wandering. Mum wouldn't have noticed,' she said to me. 'She had no sense of smell. When she was doing one of her experiments with noxious plants, years ago, some fumes got up her nose and destroyed the olfactory nerve. She stopped, after that.'

A silence fell as we thought about the events of the morning. I turned to the Inspector. 'David, when you were investigating Clifford Trent's death—you said it was suicide.'

He always says he can read me like a book. 'And you wondered if I'd suppressed anything? Because of political pressure?'

I nodded. 'It did occur to me.'

David smiled. 'And yet you trusted me enough to send me all your information. Please God, after all the Fitzgerald business, the bad elements will be weeded out of the force and honest coppers can do their job.' He looked around. 'I wasn't involved until later. My superior handled what we thought was a suicide. When allegations were made, I was asked to check again. I went back over everything but, not having been on the scene originally, there was little I could find out. I re-checked William Trent's accident and heard some of the stories, and I did begin to wonder. I voiced my suspicions to my chief. Then, suddenly, it was all taken out of my hands and I was sent into the country to investigate a murder there. I gave all my findings to the man who took over from me and by the time I came back it was all over, case closed. I had to let it drop. I was warned by my superior. He retired years ago—and, yes, Micky, has been named in the Inquiry. I was a sergeant with no clout—just obeyed orders and did what I could.'

'The system stinks,' Joss muttered. He looked at her.

'It's changing,' he said. 'There'll always be an element of corruption, but not on the grand scale we've had to deal with. Give us time, Miss Bates.'

'What about Darkwater?' I asked. 'What will happen?'

Charlotte smiled for the first time. 'Jimmy convinced me years ago the land belonged to his people. I don't think I'll ever want to build there, or live there again. Not now. I think I can come to an arrangement with the Aboriginal Council to let them use the land—perhaps as an aboriginal centre for arts and crafts. With the cave, perhaps even a tourist place. But run by their own people.'

'You know about the cave?'

'Oh yes. Bill and I managed to get down the gully when I was a child. Mum never knew, of course. Jimmy's going to take me to see it again. Perhaps you'd like to come too, John?'

'Cave?' John said, puzzled. I got Jimmy's nod of approval and explained. There were exclamations all round and great excitement.

'Bloody white fellas,' Jimmy swore. 'No sweat, you can

all have a look, but don't spread it around until we get it safe from bloody white tourists.'

Joss lingered over her coffee after the others had taken their leave. 'It's way past lunch-time,' I said. 'Can I feed you?'

'No, thanks. I'll get something from Amanda's.'

'You look a hundred per cent,' I commented.

She laughed and hugged herself. 'Recognize the jacket?'

'No, should I?'

'It's Bob's,' she said happily. 'It was delivered to the office today with my things from the flat. And a note from Joanna, just saying she was returning my things. But she must have known this was Bob's. And look what was in the pocket.' She held out a photograph.

I said slowly, 'You know, Bob always said Joanna was straight as a die and honest. I'm glad she lived up to it.'

Joss nodded. 'She must have posted them on Friday after the funeral for them to be here today. Well, I'm off. Got the final chapter of Darkwater to organize, I wouldn't dare to ask you to write it up—and, Micky—' she kissed my cheek—'thanks.'

That night I hauled Carnie out from under my bed for the umpteenth time.

'I told you, they've gone. They're going to live with a nice lady called Charlotte. Don't be so bloody suspicious.' She turned her back and stalked to her basket, wounded pride in every movement.

I opened the window and breathed the cool night air. Above, in a clear sky, the Southern Cross hung low over the city, the pointers shining brightly, defying the city lights to dim them. As rapidly as they had risen, the flood waters were draining away. Joss would get her bridge mended and she could get home again. Strange that the rain had stopped just when it could have been most useful, possibly saving

Darkwater. But then, perhaps after all this was the best way. I didn't know.

Jimmy, however, had had no such reservations. 'No more Deathwater, mate,' he'd said, clapping me on the shoulder as he left. 'Justice, mate, justice.'